Dreams From *My* Father, Okay?

The Secret Memoir of Mitt Romney

*Being a Frank and Full Account
of His Wonderful Life
as a Severe Conservative,
Classic Mormon, Sensational Family Man,
Quarter-Billionaire, and Possessor
of the Finest Crop of Hair in Presidential Politics*

❋ ❋ ❋

Mysteriously Acquired, Lightly Edited,
and Boldly Introduced

by John Sedgwick

Print ISBN: 9780786753277
eISBN: 9780786753260

Distributed by Argo Navis Author Services

For my daughters, Sara and Josie,
who've put up with a lot of jokes from me already.

And for Rana
who makes everything funnier

Contents

About the Editor

John Sedgwick is a writer and political operative best known for his revelatory *The Secret Life of Citizen Obama*, a compilation of private documents discovered in the files of the University of Chicago in 2008. One document unaccountably *missing* from the files was the future president's birth certificate. Sedgwick's innocent inquiry into the location of this missing document created a national sensation. Himself a controversial figure who prefers not to reveal anything about his own private life or background, Mr. Sedgwick acknowledges only that he lives somewhere on the East Coast. He served six months in prison in 2009 for refusing to divulge any of his sources for *Citizen Obama* and has vowed to provide no help to the federal investigation into his sources for the Romney memoir you now hold in your hands (or on your electronic delivery device, as the case may be). Mr. Sedgwick's discovery of this private memoir has already provoked outrage from the Romney campaign, which has undertaken an all-out public relations campaign to vilify him. Eric Fehrnstrom, a spokesman for the campaign, has labeled Mr. Sedgwick "Public Enemy Number One," and Ann Romney, the candidate's wife, has called his actions "utterly despicable." A rival presidential candidate, former Senator Rick Santorum, on the other hand, has praised Mr. Sedgwick as an "incredibly great American." And Rick Perry, governor of Texas, adds, "If Mr. Sedgwick can do to that skunk what that skunk did to me, I'd be one happy guy."

Introduction

This 129-page manuscript was found stored on a 16 megabyte Panasonic flash drive that was resting on a bed of cotton inside a small, inlaid mahogany box bearing the initials MR. The exact details of how it was found, where, and how it came to me— none of this can be disclosed beyond what has already been revealed in the press, as the entire matter is currently the subject of a federal investigation. Counsel assures me I can legally confirm the following: the matter did involve a German tourist, an unlocked door that led downstairs to a dusty basement, and a wall panel that swung open when the tourist brushed against it. It may further be said that all this took place in the small, red-brick Mormon tabernacle in the former cotton-growing town of St. George, Utah, that Mitt Romney's great grandfather, Miles P. Romney, helped build in 1867. (This tabernacle is not, of course, to be confused with the far grander Tabernacle in the Mormon capital of Salt Lake City three hundred miles north.)

Read a few pages of this manuscript, and you will see why it has already gained international attention and heavy consternation from the Romney campaign, for it yields a stunning new understanding of the "real" Mitt Romney, a character long hidden from view. Read the whole thing, and, well, judge for yourself. This manuscript will shift the media talk from the notion of Romney's being a "tin man" to how complex he is, sometimes disturbingly so. With remarkable candor, he discusses his tortured relationship with his Mormon faith; his bitter rivalry with his father; his many debilitating sexual hang-ups that have pushed his marriage to the brink; his pathological love of money; his resentment of all the attention that his dog, Seamus, has received in the campaign; his acute regrets about choosing Nancy Reagan as his running mate in 2008; and his aspirations to be president for life.

The issues are explosive, but the style is always refreshing—juvenile, at times, yes, but also thoughtful, humorous, quirky, and profound. For again and again, Romney returns to the fundamental questions: Who am I? and Why am I like this?

This is the Mitt Romney even Ann Romney doesn't know. It's Mitt Romney's unfettered attempt to answer the biggest question of this election year—

I.

Me

1. To Begin With

Who is Mitt Romney?

I get this question a lot, and I've thought about it a good deal, and it's an important one, quite honestly. And despite all the words that have been poured out by me and by so many others on the campaign trail, I can't honestly say that that question has been answered, at least not to my satisfaction.

The truth is, I'm not Mitt Romney. I'm Millard Mitt Romney. On that point, people have claimed that I'm actually Willard Mitt Romney, named for Willard Marriott, of the hotel chain. That's just silly. Who would ever name his kid Willard?

No, it's Millard, for one of America's most memorable presidents, Millard Fillmore, the pride of Moravia, New York, in the Finger Lakes where New York State Route 38 joins Route 38A. He was born in a log cabin, just as I was in my own campaign literature. (Do yourself a favor and look him up—fascinating man, a Whig.) And when my parents first looked down at me in our cabin, they saw a president, just as the Fillmores did.

But enough about me. Let me ask you: Who do *you* think I am? Whatever you might say, I bet you ten thous—make that a buck that it is not who *I* think I am.

I am writing this book to close that divide.

I want you to know me as I know me. But if you can't, I will endeavor to be whomever you think I am, or should be, for that matter. So please, go to my website, www.whoshouldMittRomneybe.com, and fill out a short, online questionnaire, listing your preferences on the important issues of the campaign (handguns, contraception, crabgrass) and then, in the second part, please consider the various ways I might adjust my personality to be more to your liking. Like No. 4: Should I be funnier, do you think? As a way of lightening it up a little? Or more serious, befitting the grave perils faced by our nation under a Democratic administration? Could I possibly be nicer (No. 13)? Ann thinks I don't seem very nice when I'm out at an Elk's Club of East Oshkosh Bar-B-Q and somebody drips chili on my button-down. What about you? To be honest, I probably could be nicer, but right now I don't see the point. I mean, if, say, I'm 5 percent nicer—a reasonable amount—what's the yield? What will it get me? Twenty votes? Fifty? Is that really worth it? Now, would you like to see me in your living room five nights a week (No. 17)? (On the TV, I mean.) Okay, why not (No. 18)? Am I real enough (No. 22)? Which of my five houses do you think I should spend the most time in (No. 23)? (Aside from the White House, of course!!!) Should I go after Barack Obama for being bl—I mean a person of color (No. 31)? Or should I pretend he's normal (No. 32)?

I could use your guidance on these matters, and if you could indicate your thoughts by clicking on the little circle by the characteristic or position you would most like me to have, I would be very grateful. My campaign will calculate the winners, and you watch, you will see a remarkable change in my nature, appearance, and beliefs very soon. Look out, America!

Also, if you wouldn't mind, you'll see a blue bar to click on down at the bottom of the first Web page. Each click contributes $500 to our election effort, so that I can make America more like me, and you can make me more like the person you want me to be, which is to say—if you think the way I do—more like you. That's the beauty of a democracy, let me tell you. So click that bar a few times, please! We accept PayPal and all major credit cards except Diner's Club and anything having to do with huge discount stores such as Walmart or Costco. And goodness, no cash, or those jackals at the FEC will be all over me!

The truth about Millard is our secret, by the way.

2. That Ridiculous Business About the Dog

I want you to know the *real* me, and not just another rehashing of anecdotes like that silly story about how I supposedly lashed the family dog to the roof of the station wagon for a trip to Canada. But since I am on it, I do want to correct a few misconceptions. Yes, it's true that we did drive to Canada with Seamus up there, and it did take something like twelve hours, and it was August, and it was blazing hot, but it wasn't any easier for any of us *inside* the car. An Irish setter was too darned big for our station wagon once it was loaded up with my lovely wife, Ann, and our five handsome young boys and all our stuff. And what were we supposed to do, leave him behind in the kitchen?

Seamus was fine, believe me. We didn't Velcro his paws to the ski rack. He was in a spacious dog carrier I had outfitted with a special windshield so the wind wouldn't blind him, or pin his ears back, or rough up his fur, or anything of that nature. I can't say that the carrier had air-conditioning, but we didn't either, okay?

Are we clear about this? Yes, he did "go" on the trip, but that is only natural for a dog, wherever he is, over that length of time. I actually violated our itinerary and stopped 23.7 miles ahead of schedule and pulled into the very next gas station to hose down the roof, rear window, and Seamus a little bit. Whatever that lady columnist from the *New York Times* might say, and I wish she'd get off this, he loved it up there, he really did. When I unclipped the latches to spring him, he didn't want to come down, but hunkered down on the far side from me, growling, and gave my right wrist a little nip when I reached for him, but nothing serious because he'd had his shots, and so have I. He had a blast up there. He had a better view than we did, and he didn't have to listen to the Ronettes.

And to all those dog people out there, the ones who are making such a fuss over this, turning up at my events with doggy ears and noses and little tails and howling at me all the time: you're barking up the wrong tree!

3. How Smart I Am, Part One

Now, I know everyone will want to know all the real-me stuff like where I grew up and how I decorated my room and how I met Ann—that's my wife, Ann. I love her just so much, and it is so tragic what has happened. It was when I was a Cub Scout, and she was on this huge horse and—well, I'll tell that full story later. And there will be plenty of interest in what it was like to go off to convince French people to give up Godlessness and frivolity and try being earnest, teetotaling Mormons for all eternity, and how my dad might have been president of the United States if he hadn't used one wrong word in an interview. On that last one, if I may? If he were here today, I'd tell him, "Dad, don't just use one wrong word, use lots of them, so they don't stick out. That's my approach, and I am *way* ahead in the delegate count."

And I will get to all that, but first I need to focus the laser that is me on the American people. I learned to focus at the Harvard Law School, or was it the Harvard Business School? Forgive me, I sometimes get them mixed up because I attended both at the same time. (Well, actually I don't, but doesn't it sound less insufferable this way? My pollsters thought so. And, just so you'll know, I did darned well in both programs. For my grades, see the appendix.)

Fo-cus. Don't just think about the one big thing; think about all the little things that go into the big thing, and, if you can, think of the *really* little things that go into the little things, and then scrunch up your eyebrows and bore in. You might even say, that is the big thing, all those really little things. So here—

Who am I?

Just six letters, but could there be a more important question?

Let's start at the beginning. The who. Who? A little word, who, but it is so important. It tells us so many things. In a murder mystery, for example, the "who" is the man, or sometimes the woman, who committed the murder. That's why people ask, Who did it? Or whodunit as some people say. Not so grammatical, but it's what they say. That who is the important part. Who?

Now, when I was a kid, I had a friend who said, "Whew!" a lot, and I can't remember his name, but I think of him now because Who kind of makes me go, "Whew!" Now, why? Why would I do that? This would not be much of an autobiography if I didn't at least take a stab at the answer. I sweat easily, not many people know that. And, to be honest as you have to be in a book of this nature, the whole Who thing makes me a little sweaty on my upper lip and at my temples, and sometimes under my arms and up and down my back and on my chest, too, if you want to know. (The hair there gets matted down a little when it's moist.) I have never said this before, and I didn't really expect to now, but it is so.

And I'll tell you why. It's because I sometimes see some more words right after, but hidden. Hidden from you, I mean, but I see them every time, and they make me terribly nervous. They go: Who am I . . . TO BE PRESIDENT OF THE UNITED STATES. Now, why, if I am myself running for president of the United States, do I say that? Well, I think the answer is this. My father ran for president, and I revere my father. I would be less than truthful if I told you that I believe that my father, Dad, was about as perfect a human being as you'll ever find. *Didn't* tell you, I mean. *Didn't* tell you that. Sorry. And he said one little thing wrong one time, a little thing I won't repeat because it has already been repeated a hundred million times, and Dad probably went to his grave mumbling it, and nothing was ever the same for him, or for me, or us, or anyone, after he said that one word just one measly time.* He had been way ahead of Nixon—now there's a skunk. (See appendix for the exact poll numbers.) Before he said what he said, every Republican in the country was for my dad, just about. After he said what he said, nobody but nobody was for my dad. They all thought he was a stupid idiot moron to have said such a thing. Dad quit the race, now there was a bad day, and the best he could do in politics after that was be that skunk Nixon's secretary of Housing and Urban Development so that Nixon could have the pleasure of kicking around George Romney, former president of American Motors and the handsomest man in presidential politics until me. And Dad never ran for anything again.

That's when I decided I am not going to be my dad. I am going to be better than my dad.

4. Further Reflections on Myself

All the great philosophers have asked that question, the Who-am-I one. Starting

---

* The word was "brainwashed." George Romney claimed that he had been brainwashed by our generals in Vietnam into thinking that the war was going a great deal better that it was. This did not play well with the electorate, as Mitt Romney here relates.

with our Lord Jesus Christ. And he was God. That was His answer to Who am I? I'm God. Well, I suppose the real answer there was that he was more like the son of God. But actually he was God, deep down, I mean. That is my belief. I have always believed that. I will go to my grave believing that, and I will rise up afterward and, with any luck, ascend into the magnificent Celestial Sphere—which is where all the very best Mormons end up—believing that, too.* Jesus Christ is God, but he was God dressed up for a while to be a regular guy, like he was in costume. Trick 'r' treating, say. Surprise! I love that holiday. Always went out with the kids—me in one of those plastic masks with the rubber bands. I was usually a gorilla. Ann went with us, and she was Fay Ray, from the movie *King Kong* that terrified me as a kid, only that may have been a reference nobody got since the movie came out in 1957, but we did.** Loved it.

Trick or treat—that's my kind of question, not from the trick 'r' treater, but from me as the keeper of the candy! It's the key question: Am I the kind of person, the good kind, who'd give you candy in your Halloween basket without weighing the basket, or weighing you, to see how much candy you had in there already? Or would I be the kind of person, the bad kind, who gives you the kind of candy with nuts, even though you'd told me you're allergic?

Well, I think I'm the good kind, and I think most fair-minded Republicans, the good kind like my dad, not those Tea Party nut jobs, would agree that I am the good kind, too.

But—who am I? I. That is the other little word in that sentence that means so much more than you would think. There aren't too many other words that are just one letter, and none of them gets to be a capital when it is standing by itself. I think it's because I is so skinny. It has got to be the skinniest letter in the alphabet. I is so thin, you couldn't see it wet, as we used to say in the Navy. (By this, I don't mean to suggest that I myself was in the Navy, because I was not. I was serving with the Mormons at the time.) No, heavens, the point is that there is almost nothing to I, or to me, for that matter.

Seriously. We are here on Earth for such a brief time, we are hardly here at all. I'll share this: I was driving in France one time, and a woman was sitting beside me, and a truck veered out at us going very fast. It was driven by a deranged

---

* No joke. According to the Encyclopedia of Mormonism, the inhabitants of the highest celestial degree inherit "thrones, kingdoms, principalities, and powers," and, unlike other dead Mormons, dwell with God and Jesus Christ forever.

** Actually, the movie appeared in 1933, thirteen years before Romney's birth on March 12, 1947.

Catholic priest, actually, not that I have anything against Catholics, even now, after what happened. And it slammed into us and knocked us all around. I broke a few things in my body, quite a lot of them, actually, and when I came to at the hospital, I found out that the woman who had been sitting beside me was now dead. Fortunately, she was—is—a Mormon, so she is still alive someplace. I hope in the Celestial Sphere, since that is such a great neighborhood. But do you understand what I am saying? Because this is important. She was alive and then, well, snap your fingers. Because that's how long it took her to be dead. And right beside me. That taught me a lot about life, about how it can flip over into death, just like my car did, only my car rolled over many times. And it rolled around, and stuff went everywhere, and then there's death right next to you.

That's why the I is so thin. God knows that, and I do, too. There is not much to I because there isn't. It's a hair away from nothing at all. I know me very, very well. And I will tell you the secret of me in the course of this book. It is my life story, but isn't one of those story stories that go on and on and on, like those novels I don't read but Ann does, for some reason. Mine has a bottom line, get it? And that bottom line is Millard Mitt Romney, aka me. If you read this whole book, you will know me. You just wait. Yes, you and you and you, and you in the back. I will tell all.

5. My Hair and Other Pretty Personal Stuff

I love my hair, just love it. It's so thick and beautiful and luscious, and every Republican says so, and an increasing number of Independents, according to our surveys. When I want to treat myself after a difficult day, when the press takes seriously things I said about the homeless that were clearly meant to be jokes, or makes jokes of things I meant very seriously, like my proposal to bolster our economy by eliminating taxes on anyone worth $250 million, which I know from personal experience would be an extremely welcome development for those individuals—that's when I sit at my desk, put my elbows on the desktop, bow my head, and I just run my fingers through my hair, lightly, just to feel the wonderful thickness of it, the softness of its gloss, and the subtle wave to it, as if the hair itself were saying to me: I'm not as straight as people think. It's perfect hair, they say, and I would like to agree, but that would be unbecoming, so I just blush, even though I am bursting with pride inside.

The truth is, it's my dad's hair. It is his legacy to me, along with his last name, my first name, Millard (so presidential), a $1.2 million trust fund, and his generous help buying my first three houses, for which I am so very grateful. My hair is actually a little thicker than his ever was (he is dead now, sadly), and better behaved. I sometimes think, his hair was trying to be mine, but mine doesn't have to try to be mine, because it *is* mine. His went white at the temples just like mine has. It makes for a very distinctive Romney mark, like the stripe down the back of a skunk, not that I would ever say that publicly. And it means that I could always model for an L.L. Bean catalog if the economy really tanks, as I claim it will if the Obama-man gets another four years to wreck it when he knows nothing about creating jobs the way I do.

Those cute little tufts of whiteness. They're like earmuffs that slipped. Ann often runs her fingers through them first thing in the morning when we are lying in bed. "They are so you!" she says lovingly. And it is true. Voters look at each little white triangle I've got in front of each ear, or both of them if you're seeing me head on, and they think, Mitt Romney. They do—don't you? That's me. That's my brand. That can be very useful in politics. It means I will never be mistaken for Barack Obama.

Last time around, when I ran, I didn't have those little white triangles. (Actually, I did have them, but I dyed them, so I didn't.) And I think that is why I didn't do so well. We brought in a fashion consultant, a homosexual I think, definitely Chinese, to do what we call at Bain a "retro-analysis," and he looked at me from every angle, and finally he said, "You know what, Mister Mittster? You're too handsome."

Can you believe that? Why anyone would hold that against a person, I can't imagine. Do they hold it against Brad Pitt or George Clooney? No and no. But they held it against me. It got in the way of my message. Even to me—for the life of me, I cannot remember what my message was in '08, or oh-ate as we say in politics. Something about the economy, I'm pretty sure. Jobs, maybe? Wait, don't tell me!

The white temples thing is perfect. It makes me seem much more like a regular guy. It says, look, I'm a regular guy. I've got flaws, just like that gasbag Newt and the other one, Bore 'em Santorum. The Only Living Neanderthal with Good Teeth, I call him. Who I really do not like, to be honest. The teeth. I should not be one to criticize, but I think they're too white. Honestly—do you know anyone with teeth like that? Toilet-bowl-cleanser blue, which is the giveaway they've been whitened, which says a lot about Mr. Authentic, now doesn't it?

I was amazed when that started to happen to me in my early fifties. I'm talking about the white temples now. I looked in the mirror and wanted to tell people, look, I'm turning into Dad! People probably think I painted it on or something, so I'd look more "normal," but that is not so. That is what nature intended for Mitt Romney. Take a look at a picture of my dad at my age, and you'll see.

Funny story: I may have gotten my hair from my dad, but I got my hairstyle from a wonderful guy, great friend, who worked at the Mormon church in Detroit, Len someone. So it's Mormon hair, I guess you could say. Len swept it straight back from his forehead, and I thought, "That, sir, would be a very good look for me!" So I raked mine back, too. Always with a comb, never a brush, so it would leave these teeth marks going back. I'm not one for vanity, but I will admit to maybe a twinge of satisfaction in the morning when I run my comb from my forehead ever-so-slowly back, straight back, with a freshly oiled comb, slowly, slowly, slowly over my whole scalp, all the way back to my shirt collar behind. It soothes me even to think about it—and, in fact, it is my trick for calming myself before debates, which I sometimes find stressful. It is not easy to remember all the positions I've taken on different issues over the years, or remember what pose I'm trying to strike. Whether the body-language consultants told me to favor my left side, or my right. (Newt favors his left, but Santorum is a right-cheek guy all the way, and Ron Paul always looks straight on. Interesting.) Anyway, before I go on, I sit down in the makeup room, clear everybody out, lock the door, and get a comb, and run it slowly, slowly, slowly back through my hair, and then I go out there under the lights, and in front of the cameras, and with all the mean reporters watching, and I am just marvelous.

People often ask me if I do anything special to my hair, and I tell them, no, not really. I just wash it in turpentine. I love to see their faces when I tell them that. Gosh that's fun. The fact is, my hair is remarkable, just as a substance. It's actually furry, although you can't tell that on TV. My lovely wife, Ann, says it's so thick she can't even dig her fingers into my scalp, which she wants to do sometimes after a hard day on the campaign trail, and it's finally just us, although ssshhhh about that. I wish people didn't make such a big deal of it, though. It's just hair, although there is a lot of it. It's not a symbol of anything except my virility.

6. Some Other Personal Details

I'm about six-four, well maybe not quite. I weigh 183.1 pounds first thing in the morning, and 184.5 just before bed at night, as I have ever since college. I'm regular, I'm pleased to say. I wear a 44 jacket, with a 34-inch sleeve, which my tailor tells me is a little longer than average, and I like being a little longer than average, you know? My dad was an inch taller than me, but he was only a 33. I tend to consider tailoring a needless expense. My thinking is that so long as my clothes cover me, they're okay. But Ann calls that a "foolish economy," to which I say, "There's no such thing!"

I use deodorant. That's not really a secret—everybody does, right, not just Mormons? Actually, it is the drying kind, which I need because of my little sweating problem. Gosh, I never thought I'd say anything about that. Is it just me? Or is it hot in here? You wouldn't know it, but it gets hot under the lights, and then there's talking to a bunch of people you don't know from a hole in the wall.

I mentioned a jacket. I don't wear one anymore, and I miss them: my handsome workaday Brooks Brothers blazer; the Scottish tweed herringbone one I've had forever; the very stylish Madras one Ann bought me for a trip to Bermuda one time; not to mention the top half of my suits which I have in Navy blue, blue, black, midnight, blue, Navy blue, and black. I like having a place for my pens, but the fashion consultant who came by for the retro-analysis, the young Chinese fellow who I am pretty sure is homosexual, told me I should wad up my blazers and throw them into the ocean or I'd never be president, ever, not for a million years. "Shirtsleeves are the way to go, Mister Mittster, the sleeves rolled just so." There is an art to this, I learned. First, do not use the cufflink-type ones; use the button kind. Now, primarily with third (middle) finger and thumb, roll each one up three (3) times, evenly, without bunching, the width of the roll roughly the width of the cuff, and ending up two-thirds (2/3rds) up the forearm, not half (1/2) as I had thought initially. This is manly, apparently. But I don't like revealing that much skin! Ann says not to be like that, and I say like what, and she just looks at me. I wish I could wear my blazer, cover up a little more. I just feel a little safer inside there.

Have you noticed the blue jeans? I always wear them now. Always, always. The fashion consultant said, "No exceptions, Mister Mittser!" Last time around, I was the pressed-pants candidate, and, even though I put up $50 million of my own coin, I came in dead last, and all the pros laughed and told me that if I wanted to get serious, I should forget the pressed pants, not to mention the tasseled loafers. So now I am a Wrangler man, and, I'll tell you, it does not feel right to me. My wife, Ann, whom I love so, so much, says it's because I don't have much of an a**. Actually, she used the word "sweetheart" when she told me. As in, sweetheart you don't have much of an a**. Still, it was a very intimate conversation, one I would not like to see repeated on the Sunday morning talk shows. Unlike me, Ann was not born Mormon, but she has embraced our faith now.

All I know is, I need something to feel right inside a pair of 36 straight-leg regular fits. As it is, it feels, I don't know, a little . . . loose. Also, nobody said anything to me about belts, and I'm pretty sure I should have a *whoa boy*! George W. Bush–type belt buckle like a real Republican, but all I have is my shiny, all-natural, calf's leather kind with the buckle that doesn't try to take over your whole midsection. I sometimes worry it seems too, I don't know, moderate.

Why can't I wear my jackets? Is that really too much to ask? I've been wearing a coat and tie since prep school, and forget about the dungarees. I wore a coat and tie before the Vietnam War, during the Vietnam War, and after the Vietnam War. It makes no sense: they want me to be true to myself, and honest, and authentic, and a real person and all of that, and then they want to dress me like I'm a regular guy. *Me*. Millard Mitt Romney is not a regular guy. Never has been. Never will be. Not on my watch. Where's the logic? As it is, I feel like I'm a man of the people only from the waist down, and the rest is all *moi*, as the French say, not that I would know anything about that. (The shirts are definitely me: they have my monogram on them.)

I'm sixty-five. Yes, I am. Don't feel like I am, but I am. Got the five kids, great kids, really great kids, all of them boys, although I am sure that I would have been just as happy if God threw in a girl or two, or even more. And Ann, of course. She's my wife, and gosh, am I ever proud to be her husband. I only had one rule in my house when the kids were growing up. Nothing but good, kind, loving Mormon words about Ann from everyone in it. Anything else, and there was holy heck to pay. Contrary to popular impression, Mormons are not heavy on the belt, paddle, and cane. Golf clubs, on the other hand. . . . That's a joke! I'm joking! I would never strike my child in anger with a nine iron, or with any other club for that matter. But we have better ways of scaring the beef jerky out of our kids, like threatening to send them on a ten-year missionary trip to Uganda.

II

Before Me

7. A Few Observations About the Kind of Guy I Am

You're probably expecting the part where I'm born and grow up and start to look like my father. But I need to tell you something else, first. I'm a Mormon. Yes, I am. I have the dead giveaways, the little vestigial "extra" sixth finger on my left hand and the webbed feet. Otherwise, we Mormons look like everybody else. A lot of people think that Mormonism is that thing that gives people a sore throat and maybe a headache, and then they're bleeding from every orifice they've got. But that's not Mormonism, that's Ebola virus, which is very different. Ebola came out of the jungle someplace in Africa. Mormonism came from upstate New York. Our holy founder, Mr. Joseph Smith, dreamed Mormonism up one afternoon. I don't know who thought Ebola up, probably one of those people in Nigeria that keep emailing me to send money for a fairy princess who got locked out of her apartment. Ebola is a heckuva disease, but it promises no afterlife and leaves no time for polygamy, two mistakes Mormonism does not make. Also, it may surprise you to know that Mormonism replicates much faster than Ebola and gets in far deeper in the woodwork, as it were. Look at me. I'm a Mormon, and I'm going to be president. Nobody with Ebola is ever going to be president, believe me. And here's why: if you don't get a good look at someone's left hand, you'd never know that person is a Mormon. But with Ebola, once the blood starts shooting everywhere, you can tell.

And how do Mormons replicate? Well, that's personal, but I will say that it was the Mormons who came up with the missionary position. (I am so hilarious! Is this Tuesday? I just kill on Tuesdays.) No, we breed pretty much like Presbos, but the difference is this: our patented, multiple-womb system, which was engineered for the Mormons by Eli Whitney (another Mormon, if you want to know) to deliver more and better Mormons at an ever-more-rapid rate. It's really very simple. If you limit yourself to one wife, you can produce only one new you every nine months, pretty much. But if you have forty-seven wives, as our holy founder, Mr. Joseph Smith, did, you can produce, or he can produce, or the various she's can produce, forty-seven babies during that time, and that is just in the first go. I don't know, frankly, when Mr. Smith came up with this crackerjack Mormonism idea, but let's say it was when he was twelve. If Mr. Smith started in at fourteen and kept at it until seventy-three, that could, if everything went well, produce 2,773 Mormons, which is plenty to start a cult, and might be the start of a pretty well-subscribed religion, as was the case with our esteemed faith. Sadly, things did not go quite that well for Mr. Smith, and he was cruelly struck down well before he hit his reproductive prime, but we'll get to that.

For now, all I can say is phew! I've got five boys, and there were a few tensions there now and again, despite the nine iron (I'm pulling your leg on that, we didn't really), but 2,773 brothers and sisters all sitting around the dinner table, squabbling over computer time, fighting for the remote? Just imagine the sibling rivalry! Betty wants to kill Susie because she did better on the algebra test, but Susie is mad at Billy for winning the marbles game, and Billy actually spat on Steve because he stole Susie's favorite T-shirt from Teddy who liked to sleep with it, and Steven can't get enough of Susie because of the rotten things she said about Nancy, who nobody likes because she's a little princess whom Daddy favors ever since . . . holy cow. It's like all the special interest groups in the Democratic Party.

And all those Smiths. I'm curious: Whatever happened to them? I've met a lot of people in America who call themselves Smith. And I wonder, are they "our" Smiths? The only way to find out is to ask them. Here's what I do. I look them dead in the eye, and I say, "Are you—?" That is the secret question by which one Mormon can identify another. And if the answer is a nod of the head, that means, "Yes, sir, I am, and I am here to serve you in your quest to become president of the United States of America." That is a good feeling, knowing there are so many Smiths out there, all of them pulling for me.

8. The Romney Family Tree Is a Giant Redwood, Three Hundred Feet Up in the Air, and Nearly as Deep Below!

I can recite my family tree back five generations—if I'm standing in the foyer of my modest home in Belmont, with the tennis court and the cabaña and the Olympic pool and the shrine to my ancestors. That's because in the foyer I have life-sized oil portraits of the five Romney men of my era, including me, and my, oh my, are we handsome, with the exception of the first Romney, Miles A., who really isn't, not by any stretch. You get to see that there really is such a thing as a Romney nose—mostly Roman, with a touch of Bulgarian—and we have the deep-set, romantic, Byronesque eyes that have made five generations of Romney ladies keel over from longing. The portraits are the first things you'd see if you could somehow get past the Israeli SWAT team security detail, which isn't likely unless you were

> A—a Romney,
> B—an extremely good friend of a Romney,
> C—a pizza delivery service, or
> D—a Mormon in need.

Let's start with Miles A. Romney, the one who is pretty darned ugly, especially with the carbuncle on the side of his nose and the goiter that hangs off the underside of his chin as if he were trying unsuccessfully to swallow a grapefruit. Miles was in the conniving business—cheating widows out of their life savings, primarily—in Liverpool, the famous one in England where the Rolling Stones came from, when some Mormon missionaries came through with their stirring message of polygamy for all. (Actually, all *husbands*, but that part wasn't disclosed until after the happy couple was more than halfway across the Atlantic and both parties had signed the papers.) It sounded like a good deal to those first courageous Romneys, and they decided to catch the next boat across the Atlantic and give Mormonism a whirl.

In the Atlantic, the Point of No Return is located 1,237 miles west of London, and when the missionaries finally revealed to Miles' wife the fine print allowing her husband to shack up with as many babes as he liked, but if she were so much as to gaze longingly at a George Clooney poster at the multiplex, she'd be clapped in irons as an adulteress and taken to the tower and flogged. I'm speaking of Romney's wife, who seems to have had no name of her own. She was on deck, taking the air, when the missionaries gave her the talk. She had nothing to say to them, and told them so, and then looked at her husband, Miles A., and said one word: "conniver."

Something went out of the marriage after that. They continued to breed, of course, which was fortunate because it was in this interval that Miles A. begat Miles P., and he begat Gasket, who begat George, who begat me. Imagine, though, if any link had been broken along that chain, I would never have come to be. When I think about that, I think very deep thoughts, but I don't know the right words, and can't find a speechwriter who does. Oh, I know a few—*longing* on the part of Americans in search of a real leader; a feeling of incalculable *loss* at Bain because I was not there to wring vast profits from businesses that were doing fine without us; *loneliness* from Ann, especially at two in the morning when she gets up to wander about the house and check the locks, don't ask me why; and *relief*—yes, *relief*—from Seamus, who would never have to ride on top of our station wagon. Actually, as I look back, that's pretty good! But there are more words, so many more words, many of them so deeply personal, like my own *disappointment* if I had never been born, but I will say no more. Mortality, existence, impermanence, love, beauty, death, outer space, any dimensions past the first three—these aren't my department, as anyone who knows me will tell you, starting with Ann, my wife whom I love a great, great deal.

Miles A. never did take another wife, and I can imagine why. First, he was unbearably ugly, and second, that first and only wife laid it out to him—"I don't care what the bloody document says, if *I* can't, *you* can't, you got that?"

Silence. Miles A. did *not* have that.

"Okay then, Milesy. I've got a pretty sharp pair of scissors in my sewing kit, and I know how deep you sleep."

That he got. He did not engage in polygamy, although he continued to consider it, as any man would.

When they landed in New York, God revealed his plans for them: to go to Nauvoo, Illinois, and he spelled it for them, N-A-U-V-O-O. God was very clear about how to get there, too. Follow the setting sun due west. Repeat: setting, or they'd drop into the Atlantic.

Now, some people might be disturbed to see me refer to God on a first-name basis and speak of Him as if He and I were close. But that is the case. We are close. Very. And so I speak more familiarly of Him than others might do.

To anyone who might be offended by this, I sincerely apologize, but I am not going to change my behavior just for you. Sorry. (Not.)

When they came to the Mississippi, they were to make a hard right and continue north along the eastern river bank until they hit Nauvoo, Illinois, which was well marked with signs that said, "Welcome to Nauvoo, Magnificent New Home of the Mormon Faith, House lots Still Available."

It took ten years, but those first heroic Romneys finally found it. Not much there there, Gertrude Stein sniffed, when she came around a few years later and made her world-famous remark, and the Romneys had to agree. The 1843 edition of the *Travel Made EZ for U* guidebook to Illinois, with its patented five-star system of local attractions, showed no attractions with any stars. The double-A baseball team, the Nauvoo Bobcats were still a few years off, the well-known Gangsta rappa known as [Unprintable] You, was still a twinkle in his great-great-grandfather's eye, and the Museum celebrating the Glorious History of the Mormons, was in blueprints, waiting for more history.

After a couple years of nothing to do, Miles forgot all about his wife's scissors, and he found himself drifting to juice bars in town, and worked up an online dating profile, but no one got him going, or maybe he wasn't ready. A lot of other husbands were confused, too. Polygamy seemed so new! So . . . strange, even. For generations, men may have had a few mistresses on the side, but that was different. In those days, there was just one slot for spouse on the joint tax form. This polygamy business had to be a test. Like that babe-alicious Jenny who turned lard into soap? Miles A. wanted to pop it to her but good. A bunch of his buddies did, and, seeing her get lathered up and moan-y, they were all pretty sure that Jenny was aching for it. But—was it safe? Was polygamy here to stay? Or was it like Christian Science, which only cured people for a year or two and then pretty much killed them after that. The whole thing made people uncomfortable. The men were sorry, but polygamy still felt like cheating. It was like the pill era, when AIDS was coming in. It was like God was trying to fake people out.

One Mormon who really knew how to do polygamy was the heroic founder, Mr. Joseph Smith, which makes sense, since it was all his idea. He didn't give a hoot how polygamy was going to play with anyone. He just wanted more of it. He went out on a wife-shopping binge and came back with forty-seven wives of every possible description—stubby, wispy, willowy, and plump, bosomy and not, long-nosed, knobby-kneed. Even when piled eighteen high, there was hardly room for them all in his bed.

It would have been hard to keep this a secret, what with all the cars in the driveway, but Mr. Smith didn't even try, and why should he? It was God's idea, not his own, so what's the problem? Besides, he was extremely busy with connubial bliss, pollinating all his flowers.

When some reporter at the *Nauvoo Chronicle* found out about the forty-seven, he hopped right on the story and did it up bit. The news was in big, black type across the front page of the *Chronicle*, with the number 47 in red, and then it hit the eleven-o'clock news and went viral from there. An accompanying editorial in the *Chronicle*, and three op-eds by leaders of other faiths—a rabbi, a Catholic priest, and a Mohammedan—all made it clear that Mr. Smith's behavior was an affront to decency, marriage, honor, womanhood, and everything but the infield fly rule. It was complete overkill, if you asked me. The man was just practicing his faith. If his religion called for some demonic rituals, slaughtering small children, who could possibly object? It was between him and his God, who happens to be mine, too.

Mr. Smith tried to explain that he wasn't engaging in polygamy but simply employing the Mormon's patented multiple-womb system, the better to fill the planet with Mormons. Unfortunately, he didn't have access to any of the image consultants who have guided my career in politics, and, worse, he committed a physical gaffe. A verbal gaffe is one thing. A physical gaffe is quite another. And this was his: he went at the *Chronicle*'s printing press with a sledgehammer. This was an understandable response to any newspaper's utter disregard for the truth, but it was also willful destruction of property, and it came to the attention of the sheriff and twelve deputies, none of them Mormons and none of them the least bit sympathetic.

Mr. Smith was taken directly to jail to ponder his sins until a judge could be summoned from Chicago to hear his case. Well, the locals got impatient for justice. They stormed the jail and shot our heroic founder of the Mormon faith in seventeen places, one of them extremely tender, and created forty-seven grieving widows.

My great-great grandfather Miles A. was not stupid. He could see that it was time to leave Nauvoo. And God did, too. As God had given him instructions before, God did so again. "Go about seven or eight miles south of due west," God said, "for 1,245 miles until you hit the foulest lake in America, its water so clotted with salt that you'll be able to play basketball on it, and throwing such a stench into the air you will not be able to breathe without weeping for thirty days." And out Miles A. went, in the wagon, while his nameless wife and their five children walked beside through four safely red states, clear to Salt Lake City, which was to be the new home of the Mormons, and was indeed just as revolting as God had said. But this was all the plan of Mr. Brigham Young, the heroic successor to our heroic founder, a man now best known for the basketball team of that name, who saw it as a test.

When Miles A. arrived with his family, and looked around, he wondered why God did not direct them to Palm Beach, or someplace nice. Then He might not need the polygamy angle, which had caused them so much trouble. Sure enough, there were people in Salt Lake City before the Mormons got there, "regular" people who limited themselves to one wife at a time. And they weren't any happier about Big Love coming to Utah than the good people of Nauvoo were. But they didn't just summon the sheriff and his twelve deputies. Oh, no. They called out the U.S. Army.

9. We Interrupt Our Narrative for Some Inspiring Political Rhetoric

I want to be absolutely clear about this. I am utterly opposed to the federal government imposing its own moral values on a free and upstanding people. I opposed it then, in 1847, and now, whatever today's date is. People sometimes ask, well then, what about abortion? What about the feds saying no to *that* and forcing women to some back-alley butcher or worse? Isn't the federal government imposing itself on women in that case?

That is a totally different story. Now, in Massachusetts, when I was governor, I was fine with abortion because I'd never have gotten elected if I said I wasn't. And remember, I said the *federal* government. The state government should feel free to take whatever position it wants, especially if I'm the governor, and I'm seeking higher office.

But federally? No woman should be allowed to terminate her own pregnancy in the first trimester and later if her life is in danger, absolutely not, no way. Not until the convention anyway.

You say *of course she should be?*

That's like saying, go ahead, be an ax murderer if you really want to, here's an ax. Now that I am still trying to fend off claims from the hard right that I am not savage enough on social issues, I will say this, and loudly: Someone has to speak up for that poor, unarmed embryo, and that someone is me.

Now, polygamy? You're asking, Isn't that a religious principle? Would I speak up for that?

To which I say: What, are you, nuts? Polygamy is totally out of fashion nowadays, and there are no votes to be obtained by supporting it. Now, if polygamy were popular, polling anywhere north of the 50 percent line, totally different story. In fact, depending on my own polls and my opponent's position, I might be the loudest voice for it. Or against it, as the case may be. I mean, let's be a little bit realistic here.

I will say this: Ann—that's my dear wife, Ann—would probably be all over me if I brought home another wife one evening, set a place for her at dinner, and then, when she'd done the dishes, I took her upstairs and had my way with her.

My problem with polygamy is that it's just not practical. What would the children call her? Mom? Mom-mom? Step-mom? Half-mom? I sort of like that, half-mom, but what if I had another wife after that? Would she then be third-mom? And who does the cooking? All the wives? At once? Or one dish each? Or would there be some sort of chef, sous-chef system, that would rotate, giving everyone a chance at making my favorite dish, *Coq au Vin.* (Since Mormons aren't so picky about booze that is actually cooked into the food, I like it heavy on the *vin*—if you are considering yourself a potential candidate to be a Mrs. Romney.) Where would all the wives sit around the table? We'd probably have to get a bigger car, unless I wanted to have the half-mom ride on top of the car with Seamus.

I will never, ever have more than one wife. That is an absolute with me, but if by any chance I do, Ann will always be my number one.

10. To Return . . .

The feds finally backed off, awed by the might of God that the Mormons had on their side, and we continued the serious business of populating the United States with our own kind. I don't know if Miles was spooked by the scissors, or if he had actually been snipped in the sensitive nether regions, but he never did take another wife, nor did he sire any more Romneys. But by then he had already done the important work of producing my great-grandfather, without whom there would never have been me.

He was Miles P. Yes, the Romney family goes for Miles and Miles. (I crack myself up sometimes.) Miles P. had an unusually high forehead and a bit of a lantern jaw but no carbuncle and no goiter, so he was in good shape. He was still getting children out of Hannah, the sultry vixen who was his starter wife, before Brigham Young took him aside at a basketball game and told him to quit fooling around and take another one or else. So Miles P., obedient soul that he was, went right out on the wife market again and acquired a lovely new bride, a voluptuous, Scottish lassie as it happens, and this one had a name, Caroline.

I'm not sure how that courtship went, whether it was coffee, then a burger, then a proper dinner with a linen tablecloth and nice lighting, then dinner and a movie, and then sex, etc., given that Miles P. already had a wife and ten children waiting for him at home. When did he bring Caroline around to meet the Mrs. and all the kids, I wonder? Second date? Third? And was Hannah nice about it?

Something tells me no, because Miles P. only got two kids out of Caroline before she started to sour on the arrangement. Twelve lunchboxes, twelve pairs of sneakers, twelve snow hats. Was it that? Or was it at night that she didn't like to . . . share? I can hear the arguments from here:

Hannah: He was mine first!

Caroline: Well he's mine now, douche bag!

Hannah: Why, you slut!

Caroline: Better that than hag. At least my boobs don't hang down to my shoelaces.

Then came the hair-pulling, the high-pitched screeches, the clawing at bare skin with dagger-like fingernails. Hannah wasn't much to look at—Caroline was right about that—but she knew her way around the mulberry bush, and the next thing anybody knew, Caroline had said to heck with the whole thing and vanished from the genealogical record, leaving her children behind to be raised by Hannah and Miles P. as their own.

Then God decided that everybody could use a change of scene, and He spoke up again, and He said to Miles P.: Go south southwest 137 miles to the very bottom of the state to St. George, and build me a tabernacle there. St. George was murder to find, since it wasn't near any large body of water. But Miles P. got onto the cart, rigged up the goats to pull it, settled into the driver's seat, and, with Hannah and the twelve children trotting beside, he got close enough to figure that St. George had to be somewhere around there, and he said screw it, I'm not going an inch farther. And he unloaded the wagon and found a motel for the night, and he decided to build the brick tabernacle right there.

"This is St. George, now, okay everybody?" he declared. And so it is to this day.

When he was done with the tabernacle, he noticed that Caroline had been right: Hannah was really looking her age. After the ten children, he was afraid her womb had dried up, and she seemed very perimenopausal, too. Cranky, jumpy, always carrying on about something in the paper. But twelve children left Miles P. feeling somehow incomplete, so he asked his friends if they knew anyone, and one of them said, yeah, have you ever met Catharine Cottam? She's curved like a riverbed in Zion, hollow as a crescent moon, soft as eiderdown, and hot as desert quartz at high noon.

"Perfect. I'll take her," Miles P. said, and they were married that afternoon. Then he asked, "You got anybody else?"

Somebody piped up. "My kids go to school with a woman named Anna Maria Woodbury. Ever met her?

"No, not yet. But I will soon."

And this time, rather than wait through all the adjectives, he decided to take Anna Maria to the movies that very night and then French kiss in the moonlight, and then, since it was Saturday, and Saturday was always his night, he brought her back to the old homestead. There was a fire going, and Hannah and Catharine each fingered a six-gun as they discussed the sleeping arrangements, when Miles P. came home with Anna Maria, and the two other wives were so startled by the sight of this new one that all they could do was look her up and down. Both had to agree: she was likely to be a darned good breeder. After hellos all around, Miles took her upstairs shut the door to the bedroom and, with a squeal of the well-used bedsprings, tried the new one out.

But God would not stop there. Once Miles P. had wedded Catharine and Anna Maria and was done building the tabernacle, He spoke again: Go southeast, 573 miles through the desert to St. John's, Arizona. Miles P. rigged up the wives and children to pull the cart, the goats having become stew by then. And he followed the compass to a nasty stretch of desert that was thick with migrant workers and gap-toothed farmers with Colt 45s tucked into their britches. The guns were just for defensive purposes, and, of course, were legally permissible, but they scared the heck out of the Romneys, who had not yet realized the beauty and importance of the Second Amendment, the one that says, "Thou Canst Kill Whomever Thou Wantest."

But they settled there, Mr. Romney and Mrs. Romney and Mrs. Romney and Mrs. Romney. And Miles didn't do too badly; he got nine more children out of Catharine, who acquitted herself well between the sheets, but the sultry Anna Maria kept up, kid for kid for kid, delivering nine herself, bringing the total haul to thirty. And, while St. John's might not have been their top choice, they were making due. The three Mrs. Romneys got a little bakery business going, True Loves, selling birthday cupcakes, and they had enough kids to start a Little League team.

And then the federal government swept down—*on them*. Apparently, some federal bureaucrats decided to enforce this impractical, intrusive, and insulting piece of anti-bigamy legislation—it said nothing about polygamy—on my upstanding Mormon ancestors. When Miles got exercised about it, the local newspaper, the *Apache Chief*—really, the name *Chronicle* I made up—went after him, calling Miles P. "a mass of putrid pus and rotten goose pimples; a skunk [you see why I'm sensitive], with the face of a baboon, the character of a louse, the breath of a buzzard, and the record of a perjurer and common drunkard."

But as usual the media elite got it all wrong. That wasn't Miles P.! That's Newt!

It was getting bad on all sides. Miles's brother, George, got sent to the pokey for six months because he had a couple of extra wives. Miles was afraid he'd be next, so he decided to deep six the evidence and sent Hannah and Catharine and eight of their older Romneys to hide in a cornfield for a few weeks then head up into the mountains, even though it can get a little nippy up there in the winter when it's fifteen below and the snow is as high as your head. With just one wife at home, Anna Maria, the government agents couldn't prove Miles P. was a practicing bigamist, although they must have been puzzled to see all the dresses and high-heeled shoes of different sizes in his closet, a bed twenty feet wide, and twenty-two children scattered about, all of them with markedly different features. Miles didn't wait to see what the feds would pull next. He grabbed Annie and the kids and hightailed it to Mexico. He'd send the rest of his family a postcard later.

11. A Word of Gratitude

Well, if you've read this far, I want to congratulate you. It's more than I would have. I haven't read a book all the way through in years. I've "written" some, but that wasn't really me, if you must know. I talked to somebody for an hour, and they wrote the books. But this one here, this is me, all me, from me to you. How else can I explain myself? Talking has not worked. Speeches have not worked. Power Point presentations have not worked. Glowing testimonials from important political figures have not worked. Notes from my doctor have not worked. The more I say, the less people hear. I was at my wit's end! I've focus grouped, worked with consultants, gotten enough feedback to blow my ears out. Nothing worked. Nobody knows me. Not a soul.

I don't need to be loved. I'm not aiming very high here. I don't need even to be understood, although that would be nice. I just need to be appreciated enough to get the majority of your vote in seventeen critical swing states, many of which I grew up in, live in, have visited, or own. You voters in those states, I say this to you: read on, please. It gets better, more personal, with more intimate revelations. I need you, oh, how I need you.

I have everything a human being could possibly want, except you.

12. The End of History

After Miles P. crossed the Mexican border with everybody, he hoofed it about ninety miles further before he dropped down on the banks of the Piedras Verdes River, where he set up a little colony there for everybody and set about the business of starving to death. It was all brown, the brown of mud and pig slop, like that TV show *Deadwood* my beloved Ann watched, but I never did, without the cussing. But the Romneys are a mighty people, and they got things going, and somehow Hannah and Catharine made it back with their eight, filling out the roster of thirty once more.

One of them, the smartest, most handsome, and manliest one by far, was my grandfather, Gaskell. He was the youngest of Hannah's ten, the first set. When I think of Gaskell, all I can think is Gasket, as in blow a, which is one thing that I've never done, but Dad did, a lot. With the help of Gasket and the other twenty-nine Romneys, Miles got a farm going for himself and the three Mrs. Romneys—only to find out that the Mormons back in the offices at Salt Lake City had decided that polygamy is perverse after all. But Miles P. said phooey; he had a wife shortage, and he advertised for a new backup on the sides of local barns and on bulletin boards to replace the one who was obviously gone for good. This was the widow Emily Henrietta Eyring Snow, and she seemed built for it. Good broad hips, tremendous rack, full of juice. But—nothing. She had money, though, and that was probably more useful. The grand total for this batch of Romneys remained thirty, an impressive number, no matter how you look at it. Plenty for some softball with eleven a side—with enough over for a basketball game of 5 v 5 as well, if a couple of parents joined in. Which left two refs!

Gasket was the Man. He wasn't tall, only five-feet-five, but he wasn't a headstrong idiot like his father, and unlike the others, he didn't listen to God. Early on, God told him to go to Tallahassee, Florida, then to Peekskill, New York, and finally to Anchorage, Alaska, of all places. All were out of the question. Gasket would rather stay just where he was, thank You. And he would have stayed there forever if it hadn't been for some of the hard luck that he seemed to bring his way. A band of Mexican revolutionaries descended on them, bent on converting the Romneys to leftist causes. Gasket took his family, leaving the many others to fend for themselves, and skittered back across the border to the United States without the slightest bit of trouble, since it was free of electric fences topped by razor wire, drone surveillance, helicopter patrols, alien-sniffing dogs, and fresh demands for documents every ten paces. Gasket let his five kids and one wife swim across the Rio Grande while he took the ferry.

One of the kids was the youngest, just five, already a handsome lad with fantastic hair and presidential aspirations, George Romney, better known to me as Dad.

13. We're Here

Poor Gasket. He's like me in reverse. Everything he touches turned to sawdust and cow flops. He was sitting pretty in Mexico—and then the revolutionaries with gunbelts slung crosswise across their chests come for him like repo men, and he loses everything. In the United States, he has a nose for prime real estate and a talent for No Money Down. But after Mexico, nothing seems right. He gets a fantastic little place with a mountain view, he wants ocean; he gets ocean, he wants skyline; he gets skyline, he wants to go on antidepressants. Not only that, he's broke.

That's when God spoke to him: "Go to the Land of Milk and Honey; you'll like it."

"Excuse me?"

"Salt Lake City, Utah," God clarified, and Gasket heard him say after that, "And, with your credit rating, you'll be able to buy the nicest house in town. Trust me."

"What's the catch?" Gasket asked.

"You've got to be the Mormon bishop."

Gasket responded with a four-letter word beginning in S, but this time he went along. To his surprise, things went pretty well in Salt Lake City, once he learned to wear nose clips, even when he was out of the foul waters of Great Salt Lake. He liked bossing people around morally, and his house was nice. Seventeen rooms, running water, staff of twelve.

Then Great Depression came along and caught Gasket at a very bad time. His mansion was underwater big time, since he didn't have a penny of equity in the place. He lost everything, including the two oldest, but he managed to hang onto my dad when Gasket offered the bank his wife instead.

But God said, "Hey, sorry about that, but I'll make it up to you." He did. He furnished a check, ostensibly from the Mexican government, but actually from Him. After Gasket had lost his land in Mexico, he got all litigious, as people will do when politics goes against them. He demanded twenty-five big ones from the Mexican government in compensation. Considering that would be twenty-five million today, the Mexican government said nah, but then God got on them, and they said, okay, nine big ones, which would be nine million today. God was pleased with the deal, and so was Gasket. But then, worse luck, Gasket died.

Which only shows the bitter truth: God giveth and God taketh away. RIP Gasket.

Except in my case, where God giveth and God giveth a whole lot more.

14. Now We're Finally in the Present (Pretty Much)

By the time George grows up, life seems normal. People don't get around by wagons drawn by their many wives and children, after the goats have gone for soup. They use cars without seatbelts. People don't shout from the top of one mountain to the next; they use a telephone. People don't play the fiddle any more but the transistor radio. And people gave up on polygamy and went back to adultery like before.

My Dad married only one woman, and she was plenty. He started in when he was a teenager and kept at it until he keeled over seven decades later. Incredibly, her name was Lenore LaFount. I mean, really. But at least she was a Mormon. They'd met at a sock hop in foul-smelling Salt Lake City, and then went on together to George Washington University where he won the Heisman Trophy and the Super Bowl in one season. After graduation, he went on to a highly respectable position as Aluminum Company of America's special Washington "liaison" in charge of altering legislation for the benefit of the ACA. It was in that capacity that he first coined the slogan "Yes We Can!"—a winner that was shamelessly stolen by another candidate. Through the years, some have questioned that term liaison. Others will say how if it walks like a duck, etc., it is not a liaison. And I might have been among those others if it had not been my father under discussion. A man I revere. And I will say it once, and once only. My dad was no duck!

Meanwhile, Lenore LaFount was debasing herself as an international film star with MGM. It was shameful, and someone had to save her from herself. My dad was that man. Alone in a darkened theater, watching a scantily clad Lenore in some breathy role in a Saturday afternoon matinee, my dad knew in his bones that she was not being a good Mormon. Nor was he, sitting there. But he came back and back, Saturday after Saturday, mesmerized by the shimmering vision of Lenore, his Lenore, ten feet high on the silver screen, in tantalizing soft focus.

Dad had three choices. He could stop going to her movies, he could close down Hollywood, or he could drive to her sumptuous apartment overlooking the Pacific, throw her into a gunny sack, stuff her in the trunk, and haul her back to his charming little studio over an auto-repair garage in Salt Lake City, where the putrid, briny air would knock some sense into her, and she'd give up her foolish career as a widely acclaimed, terrifically overpaid international film star and settle down to tedium and obscurity with an automobile lobbyist who wanted children.

He chose the last, of course, and Pops had the ring.

One little thing about my parents' marriage? Whom I loved beyond measure? My dad especially? They were always on each other and not always in a good way. If we had a cat, I imagine that Seamus would be a lot nicer to it than my parents were to each other. The fights of those two, my goodness. We kids would need to stuff thick wads of cotton in our ears to get to sleep. And the language! Out and out cursing! My dad was a bishop in the Mormon Church, and a governor of Michigan, and let's just say, if people knew the kinds of things he said to my mother when they really went at it, they would probably think a little differently about him. Which is why I didn't breathe a word about any of this while they were alive. Now, they're probably laughing about it, up there in the sky. I loved the heck out of my dad, whatever he said to mom. My mom, not so much.

Besides, what marriage doesn't have a few tiffs?

Besides mine, I mean?

III

Me Again

15. At Long Last

When they weren't lighting into each other, my mom and dad were making babies, and it looked for a while that they would be state champs, just like Miles P. and his various spouses. Two girls and a boy tumbled out of Mom, just like that. Unfortunately, none of the three was me. It was terrible. As they waited and waited for me to show up, a gloom enveloped both of them. Five long, sad years passed, once every Saturday morning and twice on Sunday they gave themselves over to the grand cause of creating me.

And no me.

Finally, a doctor was hired to peek inside my mom and told my mad the grim news: if this woman—he meant my mother, Lenore—gets pregnant, it could be the end of her. On a chart he pointed out some of the details, which I won't go into here, but had to do with her womb alignment.

"You mean it might kill her?" my dad asked. He and the doctor were alone together, man to man. My mother was not privy to this discussion, since it was not about her. It was about me.

"I'm afraid that's right. A pregnancy might kill her."

"That sounds serious."

That put Pops in a pickle. He got annoyed with her at times, it was true. But he really didn't want to kill her. Actually, what he wanted to do more than anything was rip her clothes off and have at her every time he saw her. He wanted her, wanted her, don't you understand?

He could not stop now. Couldn't! Every man would understand, just as every woman would be utterly appalled. And he had her, and had her, and had her again. Deliciously, enthusiastically. But ineffectually. For five long years—but still I didn't come.

And then one afternoon, they were on a cruise in Scandinavia, gazing out at the fjords from the side railing, wind tossing her hair back, the jewels in her ears and around her neck, and on her fingers all glittering, and she turned to him and smiled bewitchingly.

Husbands are wise to their women, and he gathered her into his arms. "Oh honey, are you—?"

She nodded yes.

And he hugged her tight and wept convulsive tears of relief and joy. "And you're alive."

"Of course I am. What an odd thing to say." She looked at him. "George?"

"What?"

 Why did you say that?"

"Well, the doctor—"

And he realized that he never had told her what the doctor had said.

"The doctor what?" She looked at him hard, then reared back with her right hand and said, "George, I'm going to crack you unless you tell me what this is about."

And so he did.

"You'd kill me to have another Romney?" she asked.

"Yes, I would."

She stroked his hair, as Romney women will do to Romney men. "Well, I understand. Let's face it, women aren't as important as men, and one woman more or less would never make any difference to anyone."

"I agree," Dad said. "Well put."

So everything was fine between them. She was two months gone, as it turned out, and the doctor paid my father another visit. "I'm glad that Lenore has survived having sex with you, and conceiving. But now I'm worried about the pregnancy, and the birth. George, I have to tell you, either could be deadly."

So now the onus had shifted to me. Dad had not killed her. If anyone was going to, it was me. Again, I don't know the details, but I think that I might be too big for her, and she'd burst inside, and die. This time, my father felt obliged to clue Mom in on the hazard she was facing, and he told her that if she wanted to have an abortion, he would be very, very, very sorry, but he would understand. This was before abortions were legal anywhere in the United States, even for the sake of a woman's health, but they could be had, all the same. There were always ways, especially if you're rich.

So it got very dicey between me and my mom. My dad was out of this. It was just the two of us, and it was very Oedipal. Was I going to kill you, or were you going to kill me?

Or maybe it was live and let live? Or was it die and let die?

We were facing each other down like gunslingers, but this was no corral. I was on the inside of Mom, and Mom mostly on the outside of me. I was in no position to defend myself. She could have me scraped out and dumped me down the Insinkerator, no one (but me and Dad) the wiser. Or would I get too big for her, and pop!

In the end, we both blinked. Neither of us pulled the trigger on the other. But it was scary, and because everyone was so worried about my killing Mom, the FBI was there in the ICU for the birth, and I came out with my hands up. If I'd been able to speak, I would have said, "What about me? She was the one thinking of committing a lethal act proscribed by federal and moral law."

When the feds saw I was unarmed, and there was no physical evidence of any threats—nasty letters, graffiti, forced tattoos—they had no reason to hold me, and I was given over to the custody of my parents, which freaked my mother out a little, but my dad reminded her that forgiveness is a central tenet of Mormonism, as it is of Christianity. "Even if you can't forget," he told her, "forgive." (Isaiah 20: 30–35)

"Easy for you to say. I'll never forget." And she threw the bedpan at him.

16. A Few Other Romneys

I still have the three siblings, not that there is much reason to pay attention to any of them. I think of them as Romneys who are not me: Margo Lynn Romney, Jane LaFount Romney, and George Scott Romney. Of them, only Jane puts her first name where you can find it. Like Lynn with her Margo, and Scott with his George, I have the Millard up front, faking people out. The number of people who have come up to me, big smile, and calling me Millard—well, it's not actually so many, but it is funny when it happens.

I do like the Mitt. How to put it? It's grabby. Goes *mit* everything. Fits me like a glove. (Oh, God, I'm so hilarious, I am going to hurt myself.)

I'm told that my siblings have also done things in the world, important things. Mostly, I am told by them. I can't think what those important things might be, to be honest. None of them have made anywhere near as much money as I have. Little Scotty, my older brother, tried for a political career, but got absolutely nowhere. He went for a nothing job of being attorney general in Michigan. Anybody have any idea what the attorney general in Michigan does? I don't either. Little Scotty had every possible advantage, and clonk. Name, money. I was going to say brains, but that's not it. No ignition on the launching pad, rocket just tipped over. Nada. Ixnay. Pfffft. Now get this. I love this story. So he gets divorced, since nobody likes a loser. And his ex-wife runs for U.S. Senate as a Romney, and she goes plop, too!

Well, at least I've been governor of a state beginning with M. Only two members of the Romney family can claim that. Me and Dad.

17. Dad

Sometimes, I have to wonder if this whole Who-Is-Mitt question stems from the fact that almost everything I have ever done in my life is because Pops did it, or tried to do it, or thought seriously about doing it, or failed to do it.

Marrying our grade school sweethearts, for example. I would never have tossed those pebbles at Buttercup to get Ann's attention if he hadn't gotten so flirty with Lenore when he was a little kid. Or, lately, trying for the presidency when I really can't think why, except that it would be so cool to hear Hail to the Chief every time I come out of the bathroom wearing my royal robes.

I sometimes wonder if I'm really doing it and not some ghost. The ghost of my dad. I get *déjà vu* out on the campaign trail sometimes. I'll be up at the Teleprompter or working a rope line or doing an interview and whoa! But it's more than *déjà vu*. I learned French when I was a Mormon missionary to France, and there are other apt French expressions, like "déjà heard," "déjà smelled," and "déjà freaked out by." French is so expressive! I feel like it has all happened to my dad before it happened to me, and it's still happening to him while it's happening to me. Think: he, too, was a moderate governor of home a state that begins with M; he, too, had to move hard right to gain the presidency, changing his positions on everything, and pretending the old ones were absolutely nuts. Pops had trouble faking it, but I'm fine with trimming my beliefs to fit the circumstances. What are beliefs, anyway? It's all about votes.

Dad got so excited about my political runs that in the senate campaign against Kennedy, he actually heckled Ted during the televised debates. He actually took a bus from Michigan to meet with me and gave me lots of political advice, like insisting I hit Teddy for going against his religious faith on abortion. "You can't let him get away with crap, Mittens. We'll get every Catholic vote in the state."

Everyone would go silent, and then I'd say, "Uh, Dad, that's what *I'm* doing, only I call it standing up for my convictions. It's really tracking for us. We got some great numbers there. People really trust me on this."

Then he said, "Well, how about the way the Kennedy family has buying up Chicago real estate, tossing people out the window, and counting the profits. It's outrageous!" I just looked at him, didn't have to say anything.

"Oh," he said.

"Well, hit him with health care then. The guy is trying to make health care—health care!—another government entitlement like social security. What's it going to be next? Free food for the hungry? Shelter for the poor? I mean, really, Mittens."

I stayed silent on that one, too, just took him aside and told him that the staff had gotten together and decided that we had an important mission for him. We needed him to distribute campaign literature inside all the Brooks Brothers stores in the state. "Don't worry, we'll give you a map," I told him.

Dad and I had always progressed together, true comrades, almost arm in arm. I took my first steps at ten months, well ahead of the game, and he busted out from the American Automobile Association to an actual car company that produced real cars. American Motors, a union of the Nash-Kelvinator Corporation, which always sounded to me like a trash compacting outfit, and the Hudson Motor Car Company, which seemed very swishy, to use my mother's word. By the time I was dominating first grade, Dad was AA's executive VP, but he lucked out when the chairman and CEO dropped dead. To some non-Mormons, it may have seemed suspicious to find Dad's monogrammed letter opener sticking out between the dead guy's shoulder blades, but everyone else could see that it was entirely accidental. He'd been using the letter opener improperly, it slipped, and, well, accidents happen. Dad was ready, but Dad was always ready. The body was still at 98.6 degrees and seemed to be moving when Dad had the family pictures up in the corner office, business cards printed, and bold, new strategic plan in the works.

Our house was ready, too. Even before he took over as the top guy, Dad lived like one. He moved us to Bloomfield Hills, which is very $$$$. Our place was a nice little seventeen-bedroom, with a twelve-car garage, the house cooled by air piped in from Antarctica, and a full complement of Civil War re-enactors to keep us entertained until color TV came along. It was nice, I'm telling you. The only downside? Our place overlooked the Bloomfield Hills Country Club, which meant the Bloomfield Hills Country Club overlooked it, and the occasional shanked ball came through the dining room windows during dessert.

My father wanted to join the little Saturday morning group some of the automobile heavyweights had going. But the Big Three looked down their noses at my dad, referring to his fleet Nash-Ramblers as "four-wheeled tricycles."

"Unlike those ferry boats of yours?" he replied. They were on the eleventh green, and Dad pocketed an eighteen-footer without even looking, and then chortled when Mr. Ford and General Motors and that Chrysler dandy all triple bogeyed the hole.

That's when he decided to go after them. American Motors cars weren't going to chug gasoline like sailors in a whiskey bar. No, they were going to sip gas like fine Mormon ladies at tea. Sip, sip. Pinkies out. General Motors threatened to drive Dad's "dinky" little car company into a ditch, a serious threat in those days before

seat belts and airbags. But Dad answered retort with retort. "Yeah? Try it." He was
a big man, although no bigger than me, and he rose above the fray, addressed himself to the Lord, and assured himself that God would smite them dead. But, in fact,
it was left to me, many years later, to take my revenge by telling all three automakers
to drop dead and bury themselves without a marker. Bye-bye. That sent them a
message, all right.

So the golf course was in back of the house, and it sent its missiles, as I mentioned. Then there was the front. In Michigan in those days, almost no one had
ever seen a Mormon before, aside from Mormons, so, to help educate the public,
and prepare people for my eventual presidential campaign, we made ourselves available for viewings by sightseers who came through town and were looking to see
something really different, so that when they came back home to Toledo they'd
have something to talk about. We always encouraged photographs, since my dad
knew that no one would believe that these people were actually Mormons until
they saw the "extra" digit on our left hands. Otherwise, we looked so normal! To
us, of course, we are normal, and that the "extra" digit isn't extra. It's exactly the
right number for a Mormon. Our efforts had not been very fruitful. Many days went
by without anyone coming around at all. Certainly no tourist buses, but hardly any
cars. Then—our lucky day. There was a story in the "Lifestyle" section of the *Free
Press*, and bam. Suddenly tourists were coming by the ton, many of them by those
tourist-liners you see everywhere now but back then were a rarity. It got to be that
there were so many, we limited the viewings to Tuesday, Thursday, and Sunday af-
ternoons, between the hours of two and five. And we allowed people to photograph
our left hands only every other Thursday. It would have been unmanageable otherwise, with all the Brownie instamatics. When people balked, Dad would explain,
quite solemnly, that we would otherwise be too weary from the ritual bloodlettings.
Dad would wait a second after he said that, to see if they got the joke, which they
usually didn't.

We let the tourists go through the whole house, everywhere but my parents' bedroom, which, of course, made everyone all the more curious about that. That is
how people are, especially on the Mormon tour. So Dad got quite an effect when
he snuck inside and played a record he had, "Sex Sounds of the Primates," at top
volume.

There was an Indian family across town that was on the tour, too. India Indian,
the kind that wear bed sheets. (Not the cowboys-and type.) The Basmatis charged
for visits and demanded a surcharge to be photographed in native dress. They put

up a big sign on the front yard advertising themselves as the only authentic India Indians in town, and they managed to get something in the paper, too, but the story wasn't played up like ours, and it wasn't as interesting. People had seen the movie *Gandhi,* and they knew all about India Indians. But Mormons?

You'll notice that we didn't put up any advertising sign. That's because my dad did not want to commercialize our faith. He thought that unbecoming, and I can see his point. And that's one reason why I don't like to talk about my faith out there on the hustings. I don't want people to think I'm trading on it. C'mere, everybody! Take a look! Check out the Mormon! Potential first Mormon president right here! Looky here!"

The other reason is that I'm afraid that people will think it is really weird.

IV

My Dream

18. Flying High

I'm in Air Force One, which is like a flying bowling alley, and I'm at the head of the conference table, and in my hand I've got the clicker for the Power Point presentation I'm about to make. I have all my joint chiefs around me, and a fine group of guys they are, large men with big chests that are covered with ribbons and medals all down their front. In my dream, I am dreaming that someday I'll get to wear some medals like that, after I take our country into World War Three, or Four, depending. I'm jealous that they're called the top brass, whereas I only get called Mister, which everybody is, every man over age eighteen or so. Even if, for me, it is Mister President.

I've got some people from my cabinet there, too, but they don't look like much. Newt is there as my surgeon general, a job I offered him for his delegates because I never thought he would want to go to cabinet meetings in a long white coat with a stethoscope around his neck, but he's tucked it into his monogrammed briefcase, along with his scalpel.

That's when I realized, gosh, this is not a dream at all. It's a blinking nightmare! And sweat trickled down between what little I have in the pectoral department, not like that Santorum. Have you noticed? That guy is stacked.

Paul Ron is my defense secretary, since that was our deal. I told him, "You jump on Santorum in the debates, and you can be anything in the cabinet except a teacup." So he picked defense, and I thought—holy cow, now what? But I say, "Okay, fine, Ron. Or, I'm sorry, I mean Paul since I don't really know you, do I?" And then I pulled myself together as a proven leader will do, and I said, "Go ahead, defense it is."

All during the campaign, Dr. Rep. Ron had been saying no more foreign wars. No more foreign wars. (As if there were any other kind!) Not even little wars, like snuffing out the nukes in a big, crazy country like Iran, which would never notice. In the campaign, when we were chummy, and I said, "Paul, I mean Ron, if you feel that way, you should rename the Department of Defense the Department of Defense." Parenthesis you weenie end parenthesis.

Now, I want to emphasize that I never exactly came out and said that I was in favor of changing the Department of Defense to the Department of Defense. I never if he, Paul Ron, said he wanted to, then he should. Possibly, this would lead some people to conclude that that was okay with me. *That would be wrong*. That would not be okay with me. At least, not necessarily. It would depend on the polling. Now, I certainly never ever said I'd call it the Department of Offense. That would be a bold stance, too bold a stance for someone like me. Nobody wins by taking a bold stance. No, you win by knocking down somebody else's bold stance. This is called being smart, which I am called a lot.

I do recall distinctly wanting to bomb the crap out of China, pardon my *français*. But that was an entirely defensive move, considering they were pirating *The Sound of Music* and *Singing in the Rain* and other movies my mother starred in so long ago. (I should have mentioned: Julie Andrews and Ginger Rodgers were two of my mom's stage names. Everyone knew that "Lenore" would never cut it.) This was a provocation that no man can let stand.

I will return to my dream in a moment. But first.

19. Flip-Flops

There are moments of unhappiness in a presidential campaign, yes there are. Amid all the adulation and the joy of kicking the crap out of Rich Santorum, there are times when I wish I were back at my desk at Bain Capital destroying companies in order to extract a few hundred million dollars out of them.

When, for example? When people call me a flip-flopper. That really burns me up.

When I was new to politics, running against Ted Kennedy as a male model, I thought a flip-flop was an inexpensive rubber sandal, usually employing a thong, and often worn at the beach. (By the way, that is the right word, thong, isn't it?) Back then, I would hold rallies and other public events in which I would declare my positions on the important issues of the day. Some of the people had attended previous public events of mine, where I would also declare my positions, as I held them at the time, two or three days previously. And when they realized the two positions were not identical, they would yell out this word, or maybe it's two words. Flip-flop, flip-flop. They'd sing it out derisively like basketball fans cry out Air Ball, Air Ball at games when somebody sends up a shot that misses absolutely everything—net, rim, backboard. All it hits is air, hence the term.

But flip-flop? What could this mean? So I turned to my aides and asked why people kept going on about an inexpensive rubber sandal, usually employing a thong, and often worn at the beach? My aides were not selected for their sense of humor, which you can tell if you look at them, but they thought that hilarious, and my remark got wide internal circulation.

It was my then-press secretary Eric Fehrnstrom who took me into a stall in the men's bathroom, locked it, and said. "Mittens, flip-flop has nothing to do with the beach, okay? We clear? A flip-flop is a policy U-turn. Picture your Beamer going East on I-90 and then pull an illegal 180, and you suddenly go west on I-90."

I don't drive; I am driven. So I didn't follow. "I-90? What's that?"

Fehrnstrom sighed, like he does when he realizes I know nothing about the game of politics, now do I.

"Like when you say, as you did on Monday, that you are all for bowing down to China's imperial might because you believe in open markets, and American workers are the best in the world and no one is ever going to beat us—and then this morning you say that when you're senator, China is going to get an earful from Mitt Romney because of its predatory trade practices that nobody can possibly compete with, not to mention its human rights policies, which are an outrage to human beings everywhere." He looked at me. "Flip-flop."

"Oh I get it," I told Fehrnstrom. "But why flip-flop?"

"Because you keep changing your mind, flipping, flopping, who the fuck knows?" Fernie was known to use profanity in the campaign.

I can be a demon for details; that is a large part of my genius. "I would imagine that a flip-flop is a flip followed by a flop, like something an unsuccessful circus performer might do." I glanced up at him. "Often Chinese." I glanced down again. "Like they're swinging from the high trapeze, twenty stories in the air, way the heck up there, you can hardly see this guy, and he's easing himself back off the seat of the trapeze, that wooden bar that goes across, and the crowd is starting to gasp, and he's dangling from his hands, and he's going back and forth a couple of times, building up momentum, and then—he let's go to fly through the air with a triple somersault half-gainer with a double twist, and, at the very end of it, he reaches for the waiting arms of his colleague—only to come up maybe half a foot short. Not that much, really, but enough. He plummets 178 feet to where the safety net would have been except that, in a burst of overconfidence, desire for ticket sales, and disregard of OSHA regs, he had it removed. That it?"

"No,' Fehrnstrom said.

"Fine, I get it. A flip flop is when you change your mind."

"More like you come across as a rank hypocrite."

"Okay, I said. I never thought that was a bad thing, but I can accept that. But I ask you: Does a flip *always* come with a flop? I mean, think pancakes. You flip and the pancake flops down onto the griddle with that wonderful sizzling sound. What's so bad about that? Some of my best friends *do* own NASCAR teams. Am I supposed to lie about that, and say, gee, I don't know anybody who owns a NASCAR team, why, do you?

I was wound up now, as I tend to be when a matter hits my otherwise elusive core with a pinging sound. "Or, or, is 'flop' a critical judgment on my flip. Does it say, that particular flip of yours, Mr. Romney, the one on China, was a very poor effort. A total flop. Never going anywhere." I looked Fehrnstrom dead in the eye. "That's how it feels sometimes, Fehrnstrom. I get up there and start doing a flip or two, and not one of them has ever gotten anyone out of his or her seat for a standing O. More like a seated F, arms crossed, everyone looking severe."

Fernie stroked my shoulder. Even people who are with me seem to turn against me sometimes. I can't win. In an effort to reach out, to connect, I take every side of every issue, and I don't gain people, I lose them. I don't get it. Nobody ever says to me, "Mitt Romney, sir, when you said X or Y or Z, or any letter in the alphabet, you had me. That, sir, was magic. No one had ever before been able to express about standardized testing—or whatever—what had lain inchoate in my tangled heart before. That was so beautiful. I weep to think of it. I'll never forget that moment, and I want you to know I'll always be yours, regardless of what you have said on that same subject since." Nobody says that, and *I* am the one who's inconsistent?

What did that guy in the *Dallas Morning News* call me? "Willard is slipperier than an eel that's been slathered in KY jelly and dunked in a vat of Texas crude." Willard? It's *Millard*! He makes it seem like I've ducked out on my own name!

20. Flip-Flops, Part Two: I Admit, It's Gotten Under My Skin

Abortion, flat tax, Iraq, Detroit bailout, climate change, "empty" calories, evolution, the single-wing, Galileo, manual transmission, Kung-Fu, left-handedness, IVF, raising the toilet seat, lowering the toilet seat, string theory, the planetary status of Pluto, Madonna, radial tires, night games in baseball, the iPhone 4, Le Big Mac, and the Beatles *White Album*. They say I have changed my positions on all of these, and I say malarkey. No opinion of mine has ever changed; it has evolved (Fernie says mutated, but he can be heartless when he's had a few, and I'm tempted to downsize him). In any case, it's a genetic thing. I can't control it.

Get this, there is now a website, WHSNVWHST, pronounced "Whizzen-whist" on left-leaning talk shows that Tagg—my son, Tagg—found. It stands for "What He's Saying Now (versus What He Said Then)," the "he" being me, Millard Mitt

Romney. The website is attributed to "Friends of Seamus." This I strongly doubt, since Seamus had no friends outside the family. No, I bet the Obama-istas are behind it; they'll do anything to stay in office and raise gas prices.

But take their No. 37, which has me saying that, after Seamus moved up to the Celestial Sphere, I vowed never to get another dog. I was, to quote myself, "a cat guy" from there on out.

Well, it is true we never actually did buy a cat. But you don't "buy" cats anyway. People unload them onto you, or they come mewing to your door, and you cut them a break. We Romneys did not buy a cat or take one in. This did not happen, and it will never happen in any Romney household I am part of.

Instead, I acquired a wire-haired terrier, Wuzzy, who, like Seamus in the good years, loved riding on top of the car. He didn't even insist on a carrier. But surely one can be a full-fledged "cat guy"—which is all I ever claimed—without actually owning one, if in fact "owning" is the right word for such a close and loving relationship with a member of another species. Besides, I'm allergic! We're talking seriously. I get hives over every inch of my body, and all my hair falls out. I have an inch of lab tests and a foot of testimonials to prove it, documents I have posted on our www.IllneverforgetyouSeamus.com website, given them to everyone in the media whether they wanted them or not, included them in our advertising, foisted them on sympathetic columnists, pasted them to the sandwich boards we have a couple of guys wearing on Wall Street.

But do the Whizzen-whist people make a retraction? No, they do not make a retraction. This is the world we live in today, and it is a world that is going to change in a Romney administration, let me tell you that. [Hold for applause, half smile, eye-crinkle.]

21. Oh! My Dream . . .

Seeing that Paul Ron and Gingrich were in my cabinet, I thought, God, this has got to be a nightmare. What kind of administration is this? But then I realized, no, no, no, no. This is a dream, because I am the only president on this plane. I know this for sure because I'm the only one wearing the cool, ultra-light, form-contoured flight jacket that says in hot red lettering Commander in Chief of the Known World.

And Ann is here with me, sharing the moment. She is standing beside me and bearing a silver tray of orange juice and coffee like a Pan-Am stewie from the good old days. She's wearing a tight skirt and tighter lipstick, and that smile she has on Saturday nights now that I am president.

"Would you like a drink, Mr. President?" she asks, all leggy.

"An alcoholic beverage?"

"Yeah, c'mon Mittens, unwind a little. It's been a long day."

"But Ann, I'm a Mormon. You know that. I have never drunk anything stronger than water since I was zero."

"High time," she says, in a sultry voice.

My cabinet is all eyeing me with great curiosity, to see how this will come out. Am I the kind of man who can resist coffee and orange juice and maybe something more in a public setting?

Ann gets this very foxy look on her face, and says, "But Mr. President." She strokes the synthetic fibers of my presidential zip-up. "According to the Book of Mormon, those silly ideas about beverages containing alcohol or caffeine apply only within the earth's gravitational field. Outside of it, you are completely on your own, free to make your own choices, entirely separate from the strictures of the saintly Mr. Smith and the heroic Mr. Young, who knew only of the perils of fluids stronger than water, and none of its pleasures."

"But Ann, this isn't exactly a spaceship!" I exclaimed. "It's a retrofitted 767 with the presidential seal in the carpeting and a sixteen-seat movie theater. We are bound by gravity, just as we are bound by all of God's laws, and those laws of our government that are not morally offensive, as too many of them are during the primary season."

"Well, I have a surprise for you, honey."

Just then, there was a lurch, and the plane's nose tipped up, and the thrusters fired, shooting us upward at a sharp angle. And I reared back, nearly toppling from my chair. I wore no seatbelt, since that, too, is a constraint on my liberty. Gingrich wasn't belted, either, and he rolled back in his seat and sent his Bloody Mary all over the lap of the treasury secretary whose name I forget.

"Mach 1.5," said the secretary of the Air Force, a lean, caustic gentleman named General, who'd never be able to fly commercial because there was no way all those medals were going through security. "This baby has some thrust."

Most of my cabinet is rolling around the floor, but I'm still in my seat, since I always maintain a sense of equilibrium. And then the pilot door is unbolted, and it opens, and who is it but Barack Obama, in evening clothes, looking really sharp, with that annoying smile of his, the one that conveys actual happiness, unlike mine, even though I am about the happiest person I know. When I smile I look like Seamus after our little car ride. And that dog almost bit me, not that I would ever do that to him.

So Obama comes down the aisle like it's as flat as the Great Salt Lake, and he can walk on it, and he says, "Mittens! How ya doin'?" Like he's actually happy to see me, which is not possible.

"Very well, sir," I said. "I mean, Mr. President." That is protocol between presidents, although it gets confusing as to who is who.

"Just wanted to let you know that we are out of the earth's gravitational field, and I thought you and Ann might like to join me and Joe," he gestured back to the copilot's seat, where Joe Biden was busy flying the plane, "in a martini." And he snapped his fingers, and out came a silver tray with two glasses on it, each brimming with a frothy liquid that I knew would not be good for me.

V

My Early Days

22. Mom

I want to be clear: I only have one mother, and that's Lenore LaFount.

After my mom abandoned her movie career to raise the four of us, she didn't have much to do besides pack us off to school in the morning and collect us in the afternoon. My dad was busy with American Motors, and that left a lot of hours to fill. Being competitive, she committed herself to becoming the finest Canasta player in Bloomfield Hills, which she soon accomplished since Canasta was not especially popular in town. Then it was on to competitive philately, speed kite-flying, and adult marbles. She had tried to take up skeet shooting, but there was an incident, charges were filed, and let's just say she returned her gun to under the bed, where every fearful but law-abiding citizen should be allowed to keep one.

For some reason, my son Tagg has several times now made note of the fact that my parents occasionally disagreed with each other, sometimes sharply, and occasionally threw things, although Lenore alone hit the mark, having practiced in the backyard. "The Bickersons," he has called them. First of all, wasn't that a TV show, which my parents' marriage never was, and never will be in a Romney administration? And second of all, I am going to speak to Tagg about this, as Romneys say nothing but nice things about each other.

I do recall on one occasion when I was young that I heard some words in the kitchen spoken loudly enough that I could hear them in my bedroom on the third floor, and there was a crash of some kind, as if the maid had dropped a tray full of plates, glasses, cutlery, serving bowls, and maybe a roasting pan or two. And then all of the kids rushed into my room, and it was like the scene in *The Sound of Music*, the one my mother is in, when there is a thunderstorm and everybody sings "My Favorite Things" to cheer everybody up. And we did that, the four of us, jumping on the bed and tossing pillows around. And in the morning I saw that my dad had a bruise on the side of his face. He was governor then, and he went off on a trade mission to Japan for a couple of weeks, and for much of that time, my mother had a really satisfied look on her face. And when he came back, they shut themselves into their bedroom for three or four hours so he could tell her all about the things he'd seen and done in Japan, in private.

Mom was so proud of my dad's career that she wanted it, too. And who could blame her? Being a powerful politician is the most exciting thing in the world. Making money is fun, as far as it goes. But it is nothing compared to wielding power, and having everyone admire you for the heroic sacrifice you are making by not boosting your net worth, which you never get in the private sector because you are boosting it. (Actually, what people don't know is—I actually am. I can help it! The money comes pouring in whatever the heck I do. I can't stop it. It just keeps piling up. It's crazy.)

So my mom wanted in on this, and wouldn't you know, she ran for the U.S. Senate from Michigan. Some of the columnists for the *Detroit Free Press* can be pretty mean, as I know well, believe me, and they kept teasing her, saying things like politics ain't Canasta, which she knew, and they wanted a candidate who could keep the pub in Republican, and go back to ladies teas and church socials. And the whole thing just burned her up, and she lost her temper once or twice, which is never good if you're over on the female end of things, and she got fried. She got only a few more votes than there are Romneys in Michigan, which isn't that many, since Michigan isn't Utah. There are tons of Romneys in Utah, thanks to Miles P. Afterward, she locked herself in the bathroom and cried for hours.

23. The Beginning of Me

There is nothing more boring than a Mormon childhood, even to a Mormon. No hijinks, no intoxicants, no canoodling. It is one long string of sunny, cloudless days, every single one of them 72 degrees. The only excitement was the occasional golf ball that landed in a soup plate, or a tourist who tried to slip off without paying.

Did I mention the go-carts? I had a fleet of them, all exact replicas of the cars, the real cars, produced by American Motors. In the back yard, Pops paved a track that was an exact replica of the Daytona 500, only to 90 percent scale. Word got out, and a lot of the NASCAR drivers started flying in from other parts of the country to race in the back. It was a challenge to go up against the pros when you're seven or eight, but I have very good reflexes. Most of the go-carts we had topped out at sixty, sixty-five, but that can seem pretty fast when you hit some of turns on that track, let me tell you! One time, my friend Ernie—he was a bit older than me, mid-twenties, I think—came bombing along in a souped-up BMW we had, and he flipped over the restraining wall and ended up upside down on my mom's hydrangeas. Stuck there, head down, his wheels twirling in the air. Mom was furious. Came out with a frying pan, and I sure she was going to whack Ernie with it. But no, she just banged it with a spoon to get the attention of the motor crew to haul him out.

24. The Deal with Buttercup

When I was a kid, I was brilliant at everything except sports and dating. I know what you are thinking—well, he's a Mormon, and he knows his way around the female sex the way Mike Tyson knows the back nine at Augusta. Meaning, he doesn't. But no, it's not because the girls were forbidden territory. I mean, we could look at them, and, under certain circumstances, talk to them. It's because, by age thirteen I had already selected the love of my life, my dreamboat, my without whom nothing. Mormons are like anteaters—we mate for life. And I knew from the moment I met Ann that she was my gal. I could feel it in my heart, and some other less familiar organs. I just knew: I would never dump her. She was beautiful, sophisticated, and sensual, although I could tell from the first that she needed a few drinks in her if she was going to be much fun in the sack. She was nine.

Yes she was, but all of her future attributes were in evidence except for her bosom, which I expected would take a few years to grow in. I had sisters. I knew a few things about female anatomy. And I was only twelve myself. I could wait. No need to rush things.

The scene. A quiet country road, a few miles outside Bloomfield Hills, when I had gone for a meditative stroll in my Cub Scout uniform. It was laden with ribbons attesting to my many military attainments, and, since this was unfamiliar territory where peril might come at me from any quadrant, I was packing a 32 millimeter snub-nosed Glock, capable of vaporizing hardened criminals from thirty paces. It gives a boy a good feeling to have such a piece of hardware in his pocket on a meditative country stroll.

Amazing to say, but big as the animal was, I did not hear him come trotting up with Ann aboard, until the animal emitted a powerful snort that commanded my attention. I jerked out of my reverie to stare in a sudden panic at horse and rider. I was seized by contradictory impulses (a) to shoot this huge, thundering animal to protect myself for future generations, and (b) to gape in wonder at the most beautiful female I had ever seen. The light was behind her, making her blonde hair almost yellow with the sun's radiance, and she moved so gracefully, it was as if she were in slow motion. If it had been a movie, you would just know from the way the camera lingered on the two of us that she and I were destined to exchange phone numbers.

Studly there must have gotten a bad vibe when he saw me, for his nostrils flared, he started jerking his head back and forth as if to say, "Noooooo! Noooooooooooo!" And he was stamping his hooves down heavily on the pavement.

"There, there Buttercup," the little girl said, hauling in the reins, which has the effect of jamming on the emergency brake. Buttercup stayed glued to the earth.

Right then, I threw some stones at Buttercup's head. Why do that? you may ask. It was the question on Miss Missy's mind, I could tell.

The answer is: So I didn't shoot her—the horse I mean. (I would never have shot Ann.) I had my gun right there in my pocket, and this seemed like the perfect situation. But I have, as you know, extraordinary self-control, and so I did not waste the horse as I might have, but peppered it with stones instead.

Small stones, despite what you may have read, but numerous. Ever fired a shotgun? Like at grouse or Mexicans? The shot of a shotgun isn't heavy, but if you take them all in the chest like I did once when I went hunting with Dick Cheney, it knocks you back. So. Yes, I winged a fistful of stones at Buttercup's head. I had the idea right then, it was her or me, and I'd be damned if she was going to end my presidential aspirations before I even got to puberty. People have since observed to me, when we discuss this incident. Okay, psychiatrists have observed to me that I seem to be needlessly antagonistic in this charming little story of me, Ann, and the horse. And they add that, in several other moments in the Romney life story, I have likewise depicted a situation as her or me, or him or me, or them or me, as if I am engaged in something out of Wagner. This sort of observation has given me further occasion to practice my downsizing skills over the years. But seriously, I find their remarks simply odd. Of course it's him or me, or her or me, what have you. Life is inherently competitive. I win, you lose. I live, you die. I make millions, you end up penniless in the gutter. That's just the way it is, and I learned that early, when it was I who was battling my mom to the death from inside her womb.

"But you both won," one of the gray beards said.

"No," I replied coolly. "Only I did. Nobody would ever have heard of my mother if it weren't for me."

Buttercup knew it was a beaten horse. She neighed in homage, wheeled around, and galloped off along the train tracks. The problem was, she took Ann with her. It is a fairly small town, but I didn't see Ann again for seven years, although I called and wrote and left flowers at her door and gave her presents at Christmas, Valentine's Day, and on her birthday. Since I didn't know the actual day, I played it safe by giving her a gift every day of the year. A broken watch tells the correct time twice a day, right?

She never responded. And then, to my astonishment, I saw her in the front hall of the elite prep school I attended, Cranbrook, a place designed to harden sweet-tempered Mormons like me so that we are better prepared to screw Methodists out of their life savings, later on.

When I caught a whiff of her French perfume, I was suddenly afraid she was not a Mormon.

"Are you—?" I asked, in the Mormon code we Mormons use.

"Am I what?"

"Oh." My face fell, I'm sure.

"What?"

"You're not Mormon, are you?"

"No." It was a synonym for Duh, the way she said it, which hurt. "Why? Are you?"

She made it sound like a disease—one she didn't have.

"Yes."

"Oh. Well."

There was an awkward pause.

"How's Buttercup?"

"She was rented. I really don't know."

Just a slight pause now, because my mind was made up.

"Will you marry me?"

She seemed startled.

"Now?"

"No, not right now. Later, when we're older, and you've converted, and I can support you properly, so you can stay home and keep house and raise the children in the faith. I'm expecting at least five, by the way. All boys."

Ann looked at me.

"What did you say your name was?" she asked.

I told her. I didn't ask hers, because I had it memorized. I was determined to make her Ann Romney, a Mormon Ann Romney, and now that I finally had my chance, I was not going to let it slip by. I used a negotiating trick I would later employ successfully at Bain Capital.

"You don't have to say anything about my proposal," I assured her. "I'll just close my eyes and if you are still here when I open them, I will take it as a yes. Ready?"

"Um, okay."

I closed my eyes—and then opened them again an instant later.

Ann was nowhere in sight. We were in a wide hallway, and I looked up and down. No sign of her.

I called out to her, "Ann? . . . Ann?" It was as if I was calling for Seamus, years later—"Shay-mus! Shayyyyyy-mus!" after he'd slipped the leash and bolted.

Not a peep then; not a peep now.

But in this instance, I did not give up the way I did on Seamus.

25. My War

I mean the one the Democrats started in Vietnam that was such a terrible tragedy for our nation, as opposed to the one in Iraq that the Republicans started that was such a glorious victory. I had no brief with the Viet Cong, but I didn't want Communism to wash up on the shores of California where I was living at the time. I was at Stanford U., a fact I do not like to emphasize in my campaign literature, since it is not in keeping with my present image as an abortion-hating, gun-lovin', Iran-nuke-zapping, evolution-doubting, climate change–scoffing, Tea Party–compatible Republican. When asked if I ever attended Stanford, I have, regrettably, no alternative but to lie.

Stanford students are not Mormons as a rule. They have a completely different belief system. While I believe in God, they believed in sex. There wasn't as much of a difference between the two great faiths as you'd think. At night, on the other side of my bedroom wall, decorated with pictures of my father and his Nash-Rambler, I'd hear, coming from the room of Timothy L. Brisbane, aspiring engineer and member of the ultimate Frisbee team, "Ohhhhhhhh! God Allllllllmighty! Ohhhhhh!" accompanied by much knocking of the bedposts. It was his Frisbee teammate, the red-headed Marybeth "Mab" Rand, an English major from Spokane, under him, and she was obviously a believer, too, as she screamed full-throated, high-pitched, "Jeeeeezus! Oh, Timmy. Yes, Timmy. Jeeeeeezus! God! Ahhhhhhhhhhh."

Believers, both of them, if not necessarily Mormons. It made me feel much better about my dorm.

There were several other differences between me and the non-Mormons on campus. For instance, I shaved, cut my hair regularly, fluffed up a little on top so it didn't lie too flat, with a dab of gel to get the hair at my temples to behave. I also wore underwear and changed it daily.

So long as I had my student deferment, I was heartily in favor of the Vietnam War for reasons I have already given. Would I have fought if I could? Absolutely.

Occasionally, I have been questioned further about this by members of the elite media.

"Really?" they ask. "You would sacrifice your life for your principles?"

Here is what I say: "Absolutely, sir, as any citizen would."

Here is what I am thinking, deep down inside the cavern that is my truest self:

"Well, I'd like to, but I decided it was not the best use of my time to splash around in some rice paddies with an M-16, trying to waste a bunch of gooks, when there were plenty more where they came from."

Beyond that, I figured, if the hairy-legged ladies wanted to be men, let them handle that, while I fought the real battle—to make untold millions for myself and Ann, whom I had not yet married, and for my five sons, who were not yet born.

Now, I do have a traditionalist streak. I figure if something has gone on for a while, it should go along forever. Mormonism is one example. Another is certain cherished rituals pertaining to the manly sport of football, which I never played, like the annual bonfire before the Stanford–Berkeley game, and the cherished ax that is somehow related to it. Make no mistake, this was no regular bonfire, just as the Little Boy that took out Hiroshima was no regular bomb. If you could take a Saturn V rocket, invert it, and bury it straight down so that its tail was flush with the ground, and then hit the blastoff button, you would have a rough approximation of the ritual bonfire before the Stanford–Berkeley game. We set up this four-story pyramid of federally protected giant redwood logs, doused it with a petroleum product that has done more than its fair share to increase global warming—which does not, repeat not, exist—and all it needs is somebody with a lit kitchen match and good set of wheels—because that baby does a real ka-BOOM.

Well, my freshman year, some of the boys and I got advance word that some Berkeley hooligans were planning to sneak onto campus incognito with a kitchen match and set off our Roman candle a little early, hah hah hah. Worse, they were planning to snatch the ceremonial ax—a broad red blade that, according to legend, a Norseman had used to behead another Norseman—that went to the winner of the game.

Fortunately I was on the Ax Committee, or Ax-Com, as we said. President of it, actually. (I'm blushing now.) Okay, maybe there was nobody else on Ax-Com that year. But I took it upon myself to protect one of the most sacred traditions on campus, or what would be next? As soon as I learned about this dastardly plot, I designed and then donned an Ax-Com uniform, with epaulets and ribbons of valor, and got out my cardboard M-16 and, with the gun smartly on my shoulder, I marched about the perimeter of the log-pyramid zone and also the secret location of the Ax, which will not be revealed here, but which was not in the same place, and so I couldn't be both at locations at the same time. So I was running back and forth, back and forth with the cardboard gun, and some sweat was starting to soak through my chemise in the underarm and chest areas. Now, you may laugh, but I took this very seriously, and I won't apologize for that, or join in the laughter.

Then I remembered Communism and how that was eradicated. It's like Kudzu. You cannot wait for the twigs and leaves to come engulf you, or it's too late, you'll drown in the stuff. You have to track it back to its roots, and chop! Get it before it gets you. This is one of my personal maxims; it has never steered me wrong.

So, this was the plan: go deep undercover, infiltrate the Berkeley campus, identify the potential ax-snatchers and bonfire burners, and take them out.

This was the problem: Stanford might be left, but Berkeley had left the planet. Kids wandered around naked, smoked marijuana in biology class, drank LSD with their orange juice, dropped their g's, gave their parents the finger, and refused to consider high finance as a potential career. In this setting, I was afraid that my chinos and penny loafers would give me away. So I put on some blue jeans from my friend Stuart who sometimes wore such things on the weekend, and wore some bathroom slippers, a ripped-up undershirt I should have tie-dyed and a purple cowboy hat, and I hailed a cab to Berkeley and had the driver leave me off several blocks from campus, so I could roll around in some puddles and dirt before I appeared on the hallowed ground of UC Berkeley.

There, for four solid days in the sultry late spring air, I wandered about, feigning an acid haze but actually keeping my eyes peeled for anyone carrying a match or a pair of woodsman's gloves for handling an ax without getting blisters. I saw no such person, in truth, although I felt a lot of warm gazes from half-naked ladies on campus, who fell for my Roman nose, with just a hint of Bulgarian, and my gorgeous, but unusually short, hair. Even though I intercepted no foreign agents, my mission over those four crazy days and nights was successful. The bonfire went up on schedule, the holy ax was safe, and Stanford shut out the Berkeley pussies 20–0.

If there had been other members of the Ax-Com to give me a trophy, I would have proudly accepted it from them, but as there was not, I presented it to myself with admiration and gratitude, and I received it that way, too.

26. An Early Brush with Fame

Few people now remember a radical activist named David Harris; many more are aware of me. He was one of those left-wing activists who cause a storm and fury for a time, but they never amount to anything. They are not like me, who never causes a storm and fury, but you are reading about me now. If Harris was famous, it was because he went on to marry the warbly voiced folksinger Joan Baez, her last name pronounced in two syllables, to rhyme with prayers as pronounced Mark Huckabee in full drawl. Harris had this idea that if he and some of his hairy, no-underpants types picketed the Stanford administrative offices, President Nixon would just give in and let Ho Chi Minh have all of Southeast Asia, and he might throw in India, too.

I was staunchly opposed to this adolescent gambit. I had my student deferment, as I say, and I saw no reason to give up on the Vietnam War, not so long as (a) America's defense contractors were still in business and (b) we had a chance at getting those enemy combatants to buy our Cokes, Marlboros, Big Macs, and Kodachrome once the hostilities were completed.

After saving the ax, and the bonfire, I was on a roll, and I was ready to take on my toughest assignment yet: keeping the Vietnam War going for another generation, at least. Berkeley may have surrendered to the Viet Cong, but I had to save Stanford, or the dominoes of doom would tumble. There was not a moment to wait. I could already smell the marijuana in the cafeteria and see the National Liberation Front flags hanging out of dorm windows. The communist threat was rising, day by day.

That David Harris ran for student body president against six handsome, articulate, sensible frat boys, and, unkempt as he was, he did a number on them. It was scary to see what a strong message, fully felt and powerfully articulated, can do. Wow! Imagine—if I had just a handful of something like that. . . .

So David Harris had taken Stanford University, and now he wanted the whole country. I just knew he was going to run for president one day. One presidential aspirant can smell another; there's something in the pheromones. I had to stop him—now—or I'd be doing battle in Iowa City when he had millions of longhairs behind him. In one of his first acts as president of the student body, he launched a massive peace protest, urging an end to the war, and a withdrawal from Vietnam. It was absurd. He handled it like a march on Washington, which no doubt he was preparing for, except it was aimed not at the White House but at the administration offices of the Stanford president, Carl Jones.

I was determined to let the world know that Stanford's students certainly did not speak with one voice on that issue, and David Harris did not speak for me. In fact, I was hoping people would come away with the idea that he spoke for nobody except David Harris. Let him have the slobby, bedraggled set who ran about with their breasts untethered and their nose hair unclipped, I put on my pressed chinos and clean underpants and a very smart button-down shirt in a flattering pale blue and then topped the whole thing off with my Cranbrook blazer and $37.50 haircut.

Then I created my own message. On a sheet of cardboard from the laundry, stapled to a high pole, I wrote, in bold red, "WE WANT WAR!!"

And then I went out to join the parade. At first, the radicals thought my protest was some kind of a joke, a parody of the whole "jerks for Jesus" crowd. But I caught David Harris's eye when he was up there with a microphone, going on about American imperialism, which he was against. When he saw me, he could tell I meant business. A presidential candidate can always spot another. And he saw me, and he was awed. He had his crowd that day, and I didn't have mine. But look at us now.

After that he married Baez, but then he went to jail for draft dodging while I got a deferment for being a Mormon. When he got out of the jug, she dumped him. Now, I wonder why? I don't think those anonymous letters I wrote to her about him had anything to do with it, I really don't. By then, I was in France, dreaming sweet dreams about Ann, my fiancée to be. And now? David Harris is a nobody nowhere, and you're reading all about me.

VI

My French Years

27. The Letter

If you're lucky enough to be a Mormon, at some point you get a letter. It tells you where in the world you should go to save people from whatever religion they might have, if they have any, and bring them into the warm, milky bosom of Mormonism, which will make them happier and more fulfilled than they would ever have imagined a religion that proscribes alcohol and limits sex could ever do. But it has done this for me and Ann, now that she has converted and had the extra-digitization surgery, as we call it, my five handsome sons, and every other Mormon I know. It's a service that we Mormons have been providing mankind ever since our holy founder, Mr. Joseph Smith, thought it up that brilliant summer afternoon in 1847.

Incredibly enough, many people, even after they read the brochures and watch the video, don't want to become Mormons. I don't know why, quite honestly, and our marketing people are working on it. I've looked at it from a business standpoint, and I'm convinced there is absolutely nothing wrong with the product. Even if we can no longer offer polygamy, we do guarantee eternal life, and that is a pretty sweet deal. Again, just look at me and Ann and our five handsome, well-adjusted sons and all the houses we have. Who would not want to be us?

There is the little matter of the two years of missionary work, however. I was a little worried when I opened up my Stanford mailbox and saw the fat envelope from a Richard. T. C. Lankton, Chief, Missionary Division, Mormon Church of Latter Day Saints, Salt Lake City, Utah. I held it in my hand for a little while, staring at it, flipping it between thumb and index finger, since my future was inside. I could be sent anywhere on earth—outer Mongolia, Zagreb, Dubai, San Francisco.

But no, I shut my eyes, ripped open the envelope and—France! Ooh-la-la, as Timothy L. Brisbane told me before he disappeared into his bedroom for one last round with Mab before Frisbee practice. I didn't know what to think. I'd never been to France, never been out of the country at all except on ski trips, cruises, and grand tours of various continents. I spoke a few words of the native tongue (I recall one: wee, which is French for yes), all of them with a Mormon accent, which is a little flat on the A's, and I knew all about French culture—the Moulin Rouge, Napoleon, Crêpes Suzette, za vay zay zay zis and zat with two fingertips pressed against their opposing thumb-tip like a chef who is going on about the vichyssoise. But after I looked up France in the encyclopedia, three things troubled me:

1.   They did sex
2.   They did cigarettes
3.   They did wine

There comes a time in the development of every potential world leader when he is tempted by pleasure. It's true. I speak from experience. How could this be, you ask? What's it like to think of pleasure as a temptation, and not just something to have? While this is something that every potential world leader knows, it is something he rarely speaks of, so let me explain. Imagine you're in the desert, and a fellow comes up to you with his hands out and his fists closed. In his left hand, he says, is every delight that a man can have, leaving none out. And in his right hand, he says, is every duty a man can have, leaving none out. Whichever hand you pick, you cannot have so much as a flyspeck of the other. It's all or nothing. Choose duty, and duty is all you get. Choose delight, and you get only delight.

So, sir, choose. What'll it be?

Every potential world leader worth his salt picks the duty hand, and duty is all he does, forever after. If he should happen to experience pleasure, it would be, for him, a duty. For the potential world leader is not a hedonist, although he is sometimes a philosopher. But only sometimes, since potential world leaders have little time for philosophy.

Back to the two fists. I chose duty.

France is a big place with a lot of pleasures in it. Every corner of the country was stocked with them, and they worried me a great deal. I'd have a Mormon roommate to keep an eye on me, and vice versa, but still—. At that point, my future, lovely wife, Ann, was just a sophomore at Bloomfield Hills High School. Before I flew off to my new life in La Belle, France, I took her out for a milkshake and stroll through the mall. And I noticed something: she was wearing a bra. She was developing. I could see the slender white strap where it pressed tightly into her shoulder. When I left to pursue my destiny across the Atlantic, I looked Ann in the eye, shook her hand, and began, "Ann Davies—"

"It's Ann," she interjected. "You don't have to use my last name. I know it."

"Of course." As a potential world leader, I was not rattled, but carried right on.

"Ann, in two years, when I've finished my tour of Mormon duty in France, and turned as many French people into Mormons as I possibly can, I'm coming back here to Bloomfield Hills. At that point you will not yet be eighteen, although I will be twenty-one and ready to move to the next stage of romance. I will drive to your house in an American Automobiles automobile, knock on the door, and hope you are in. If you are, I will say hello and ask you to go for a walk and maybe take in a movie, and I will fill you in on my adventures in La Belle, France, as they call it. With your permission—"

"But—"

"Please don't interrupt. When you actually are eighteen, I am going to upgrade, and call first to ask you out, and if you accept, I am going to come to your door in a slightly more expensive late-model American Automobile, and I will open the door for you, settle you inside, and come around to the driver's seat, and then, with your permission, I will kiss you." I waited. "Any questions?"

"And if permission is not granted because you're such a big fucking dork, then what?"

That took me aback. "Well, I guess we'll have to deal with that when the time comes."

Four thousand miles away, in Paris, there would be no Ann, only the idea of Ann. Ann of the feathery eyelashes and the voice like melted butter. That was plenty for me. Ann was then what she is now and will always be—my honey bunny, my mizzy wunki, my zoo zoo zoo zimpikins. I love her to death, and beyond. I knew I would spend all eternity with her, in the Celestial Sphere, if we should be so lucky. It was a serious commitment, mine.

But while she was in Bloomfield Hills, I was in France. One of those challenges God has occasionally thrown in my way to see how I'll handle it. I was in Le Havre, to be exact, on the English Channel, which means the French up there were not the French you hear about, the ones down by the Mediterranean, the ones who lie naked on beaches, fornicate in the back seat of Citroens, drink, flock to Cannes, and are unlikely to want to be Mormons. But the climate was so rotten up north, so moist that a strange film started to appear on my foot webbing, which I did not dare take to a doctor, for obvious reasons. It cleared up after a year or so, but it was a message. It said: everything is so bleak and miserable in Le Havre and environs, that surely people hereabout would go for the inspiring message of Mr. Joseph Smith and Mr. Brigham Young about how great life can be if you're Mormon.

I thought we had a good product, I really did, but when I went door to door, the husbands kept asking me about only one thing.

"*Mais le polygamy?*" they would ask hopefully.

I'd shake my head. "*Non, non monsieur. Pas encore.*" I'd learned a few words, the ones that kept coming up.

They'd ask this quietly when their wives were in the kitchen, where wives quickly went when I came around. Even though I'd only mentioned the polygamy as an example of how Mormonism 4.0 was a much better religion than the previous versions, I could see from the way the men's faces fell practically onto the carpet that they were disappointed. And then, when they learned they had to hand over a tenth of their income, *and* give up drinking, they said one thing.

"*Merde*," which is French for chop suey.

This was a hard moment in the sale, and I should have handled it better—as I did later in my career in the deceptive arts, during my first televised debate with Teddy Kennedy, when, thundering with indignation, he asked me how I could send hundreds of women to the guillotine and allow thousands upon thousands of tiny infants to starve just to make a few hundred million dollars for Bain Capital, of which I would personally take home 93 percent.

I'd had that scalp rubdown. I was calm as calm could be. "Well, Senator," I said, "some of us have to work for a living."

That was a beautiful moment. I saw the tape afterward, and it looked like somebody had socked Kennedy right there in the colossus mid-sectionus.

But I was a newbie there in Le Havre, and I had nothing.

"You have me there, monsieur," I said. "Perhaps I should leave now, so you can slam the door behind me?"

When I went over there, I brought my French phrasebook, two years' supply of clean underwear, a magnum tub of brill cream, which you can't get over there, two envelopes for the annual letters I was allowed to send Ann, and the addresses of all the McDonald's in the city. Teach a man to fish and he has fish for—how does that go? If anyone should ever question if there is a Mormon god, Big Macs are the proof. Think about it: everywhere in the world a Mormon missionary might go to convert some unsuspecting Mohammadan, the golden arches are there, raise their glowing yellow bars heavenward, and make Quarter Pounders available with fries and a large Coke to pale and saintly émigrés from Utah for a reasonable price.

Forgive me, Lord, if I blaspheme, but in a land of heavy sauces that give me gas, a Big Mac is juicy manna, and proof of the love of the almighty, not that the issue was ever in doubt with me, even after the 100,000th door was slammed in my face and/or rear by Le Havrians, who, outraged by the non-polygamy, held me personally responsible for the murder of innocent gook ladies in Vietnam, Cambodia, and even Laos. They would not even listen to one *mot* of my message of hope, peace, and love.

I could tell you a few things about getting a door slammed in your face and/or rear. Each one is different. I found that the heavy-set hausfrau type was the one where you really had to watch out for. They get this look before they grab the door handle and go into their windup. That's your cue to step back in haste. My friend, Teddy? From San Diego? Too slow. He broke his nose in two places and had to be medevac'd out of there. I believe you can still see the blood on the door at 45 Rue de Finis.

A sign.

I did convert one elderly man in a beret, which got some of the guys pretty pumped up back in the missionary office. "Scorrrrrrrre!" one telegrammed back. But for the entire first year, it was just that one.

28. Meanwhile, Back Home

Dad was engaged in a similar effort, except that his was with Ann.

Tell you the truth, I was a little alarmed when I heard that he was spending so much time alone with her, but I was limited to just annual letters home, too, and had to wait nearly a full year before I could tell him so. He told me all he was trying to do was convert her. Because of the delicacy of the work, he didn't not try to handle it all by himself, just as no brain surgeon, no matter how brilliant, will not perform brain surgery solo.

Dad brought in a conversion expert. No, a legend. Signor Jorge Piñata. He had personally converted 273 Filipinos in a four-hour event in an indoor soccer stadium in Manila.

No one in Ann's family has ever been Mormon, and, except for Ann, they responded to it the way Buttercup had to me. In the first few weeks of the conversion, Dad and Jorge had to spend a lot of time debunking certain myths regarding ritual flogging and mass suicide, and to correct them on the subject of broccoli, which *is* permissible. (The others are not.) Dad was governor of Michigan at the time, and he was running for president. More importantly, he'd cured some kid who had polio. Dad patted him on the head one morning, and that afternoon the little guy was playing Little League. The story got into *Life* magazine, and made quite a splash in those days when only viruses could go viral, but he still received get-the-heck-away-from-us looks from Ann's parents when Dad entered the living room and started to approach Ann where she was lying back on the couch.

There was an amusing part of this. Somebody told somebody of Ann's interest in Mormonism, and word spread around the neighborhood like that telephone game, until it reached J. L., a high school freshman and Seventh Day Adventist who must somehow never have heard of Mormonism; he thought Ann was interested in Onanism, which every SDA can define. We had a telephone in those days, and kids used it, and, boy, I am embarrassed to say that drew a crowd. Kids were ringed three deep around the house the evening my Dad and Jorge went in for the next lesson. I don't think my dad could see the kids outside, because the light reflected in, but they were out there, staring quietly. Ann's parents only let in one outsider—the girl who was going out with Ann's brother, who'd hit puberty by then. When she heard about the Onanism, she had to go to the dictionary and came back blushing, which meant she would make a good Mormon. Finally, when Dad and Jorge took a break before the ritual measuring of the left hand, Dad saw everybody on the lawn outside, and, when he found out they were not there to be Mormons, he sent them away with a big, booming voice. He did not want to hear a word of what had drawn them there, although he did anyway. They never came back.

Ann's little brother wanted to hear the good news, too, but Ann's parents said, absolutely not! So he listened through the door and took notes to pass around to all his friends in the sixth grade.

It took six sessions, but Ann was a quick study. When she could recite the *Book of Mormon* in three languages, including Elvish, Dad clapped her on the back, and said, "You're in."

"But what about the Onanism?"

Dad was not thrown by such questions. "For that, you're on your own."

Dad baptized her himself. I wish I had been there for her ritual plunging into the baptismal font, wearing only some light cotton woven by blind Mormons in Argentina that is somewhat translucent when wet. Her friend, Cindy, wanted to get baptized in her bikini, and I would certainly have liked to be there for that, but her father said, what was she, out of her mind? Little Jim went through with it in snorkel gear. This gave Dad two converts, but at that point I had seven. Confirmed ones, I mean. Lots of people will say, "Sure, sure, of course I'll be a Mormon," just to get you out of the house. But are they really Mormons? Have they accepted Jesus Christ as their personal savior and given up schnapps? That's where the follow-up surveillance team comes in, but I digress.

29. Dad Again

This part is sad. Has it ever happened to you that someone you revere almost as much as you revere God completely blows it, and ever afterward, even though you tell everyone that you still admire the heck out of him, you actually don't, really, not so much? This has happened to me. It involves my dad. Did I mention that he was six-feet-eight, weighed more than 260 pounds of solid muscle, and could bench press a VW Microbus? He was captain of the football team all four years of high school where he played first chair on the chess team, or was it violin in the state orchestra; went on to George Washington University, where he was accepted by acclamation and led the football team to an unprecedented four undefeated seasons; and he himself, as quarterback, won the Heisman Trophy and a Rhodes Scholarship, which he declined out of deference to the Mormon religion, which sent him to Manitoba to convert Eskimos.

It was a lot for me to live up to. And this was *before* he was three-time International Executive of the Year as an automobile lobbyist in Detroit, created American Motors, and made it such a powerhouse that the Big Three became the Big One, Baby, and his anti-gas-guzzler crusade was so successful it reduced the fleet mileage of all American cars from more than 42 miles per gallon to a little less than 53 miles a *cup*. I was only twelve, but I told him that, with a résumé like that he should run for governor.

"But as what? A Democrat? Republican?"

"As a Romney, for goodness sake. The Romney Party! You don't have to stand for anything, just be yourself. Everything else, just make it up as you go." You know what? I think he secretly wanted to be a Democrat. He had this ridiculous idea that Democrats were all about *improving people's lives*! I had to walk my dad through this very slowly. People? Who's people? Beyond corporations, I meant. Rich people, I nearly screamed at him. Rich people! Even then, I hated the defensiveness of the rich, constantly surrendering their rights and privileges to lead lives far better than anyone else's. That's number one. And, as proof, I said, "Look in the mirror. Aren't you people? Now, look at Mom and me. Aren't we people?"

Having just been elected president of my class, I knew my way around politics. The trick is you just say whatever you need to. If you want Betty's vote, you just say, "Betty, you are the prettiest girl in the class, and I am dying to kiss you on the cheek, except it is prohibited by my religion." And she goes, "Ohhhh, Mittens."

Then you go to Liz, and say, "Liz, you are the prettiest girl in the class, and I am dying to kiss you on the cheek, except it is prohibited by my religion." And she swoons, too, of course.

And then you go to Bill, and you do not say, "Bill, you are the prettiest boy in class, and I am dying to kiss you on the cheek, except it is prohibited by my religion," because my religion has nothing to say about that, considering it so unlikely. Instead, you say you'll give him a dollar.

This is the art of politics.

I campaigned all over Michigan for my dad—in the thumb part of the state and the whole rest of the mitten, too. I own Michigan. I killed in Michigan. I left them rolling in Michigan. Everywhere I went, I'd shout, "Vote for my dad! He'll be the best governor ever. He'll cut your taxes, eliminate waste, slash the Medicaid rolls, and improve services in your neighborhood and at your country place, too!" If they wanted issues, I'd ask them what they wanted to hear. If they said we're for guns, against abortion, and right down the middle on the Vietnam War, I'd say, "Why, so's my dad!" And they'd cheer wildly.

If at the next stop, they'd say we're against guns, for abortion, and upside down and backward on the Vietnam War, I'd say, "Why, so's my dad!" And people cheered that wildly, too. That gave me my first major insight into politics. People don't care what you say, so long as you're handsome and you agree with them. Dad was so handsome, I saw men everywhere started dabbing a little white on their temples. He was elected, and then elected again, and I think he'd still be governor of Michigan if he weren't, unfortunately, dead.

So now we're coming up on 1968, an election year, and Dad was raring to go for the brass ring. An observation, if I may? Politicians are like rockets. They can only go up. They're dog catchers; they want to be dog groomers, and so on up to the presidency of the United States, the very top position of all, which I am now seeking myself. Early polls had Dad creaming Nixon, and LBJ, too. But this was a messy time, and there were race riots in Detroit, and unfortunately Detroit is part of Michigan, and Dad thought he should do something. I knew all about the plight of black people from our two maids, not that they ever said a word about it. They bore their plight with such majesty. Is that the right word? But, my goodness, were they ever black! Dad didn't want black people burning a lot of cars and making a mess killing each other, although it seemed fine to me if that was what they wanted to do, and he asked LBJ to send in troops to settle everybody back down. LBJ took his time about that. There was only about half of Detroit left when the troops got there, and Dad wasn't quite as popular as he'd been. LBJ nosed ahead of him in the polls, although Dad still had the edge on Nixon. But I gave Dad some advice. Since you care about Detroit so much, I said, maybe drop the trip to the French wine country until the city stops smoldering? And by the way, aren't you Mormon? Are you supposed to spend six weeks in French vineyards? France will always be there, and Detroit might not be—and didn't you used to work in Detroit? Maybe you have friends there? And Dad said, oh, okay. And his poll numbers went *boing*, straight up; people were impressed he would give up a couple months lounging about France to pursue the presidency.

And Dad was feeling so happy about things, and so relaxed, that he went and did that interview with a lightweight named Lou Gordon, who had the audacity to ask about Vietnam, and Dad said that one silly word, and this titan of a man was not going to be President Romney.

I am.

30. Paris, France

This is when that woman died on me. Leola Anderson. I still remember her name. The wife of Duane Anderson, the president of the Mormon mission in France, who was also in the car. There were student riots in Paris, and, being short on Mormons, society was really breaking down, almost as desperately as in the United States, which not only had riots, but also had assassinations. I was Duane's assistant, and I drove him around in the official Mormon Citroen DS. Duane's job was to keep all the Mormons in France happy, which wasn't too hard since there couldn't have been more than a couple dozen of them. And when word came down that a couple of elderly Mormon ladies in the South of France were calling each other names, we hopped right on it, and in seconds we were on the Interstate headed south. We overnighted there and took care of the two old ladies in the morning. They were sobbing in each other's arms when we left, another job well done. It was a full car, actually. Not just the two Andersons, but also a Mormon couple from Bordeaux, and a nomadic Mormon named David Wood, all three jammed into the back.

God speaks to us in mysterious ways, but if we just listen, we will hear His message. Well, I wasn't listening that day, although he was screaming at me—Look out for God's sake! For just as we driving through the town of Beaulac on a two-lane highway, we came upon what was left of a real crack-up. Somebody had slammed into a tree and, in those days before seat belts, had been propelled through the open roof and way up into the trees someplace. The car was there, all mangled and steaming. But the driver was just . . . gone. Strangest thing.

So we kept on, as people will, even in the face of God's warnings, and I'd hardly gone twenty meters before the deranged Catholic priest swung around into our line and smashed head-first into our car.

This was the weird part, even aside from Leola's flipping around with me like a couple of socks in the dryer and her ending up dead and me not, her husband, good

Mormon that he was, never got over it. He was never able to get all the way through the five stages of grief but kept getting hung up on one of them, and had to go all the way back to start over. He did the denial just fine. He insisted Leona was still alive, just vacationing in Miami. I really didn't have the heart to tell him anything different But then he'd get angry—well, more like pissy, really. He'd say things like, "Mittens, why didn't you sit in the goddam middle seat?" Then the bargaining, "Mittens, I've been thinking: How about you go kill yourself, so I can get Leona back?" Then, just when he should have gotten to acceptance, it was back to denial again. He was sure Leona was in Miami. But then she didn't call, or write, or come back, and that bumped him ahead to depression, and we were all excited that he was almost there, almost to acceptance—and then more pissiness about why I had to go on that stupid road anyway, and didn't I know it was a sign when that other driver disappeared into the trees.

That was one of the few times I have questioned my faith. How could a just God make a good man like Duane Anderson so mad at me? Was He pissed at me, too? I would never have imagined it, but a couple of months later, I was in a Peugeot negotiating the narrows streets of LeMans, famous for its car race, and I was proceeding extra cautiously, as I had been ever since the Citroen crash, and this time I looked up into my rearview to see an immense garbage truck charging toward me, filling up the rearview. I braced myself, and sure enough, the thing plowed into me, and then I hit the car in front, and it hit the car in front, just like the dominoes going clink-clink-clink-clink in Southeast Asia. After that, I told the Lord I was done with French drivers, and He agreed.

VII

Back Home

31. On Being So Smart—Part Two

Want to know how smart I am? Of course you do. Right now it is a national fascination. The whole country is wondering how a man like me, who seems to a few people—liberal people, I might add—to be nothing but hot air, as my mother used to say of certain salesmen who would come to the house offering steeply discounted vacuum cleaner bags, could be on the verge of winning the Republican nomination for president. The answer is, I am really, really smart. I can see around corners, imagine worlds that do not yet exist, and multiply seven-digit numbers in my head.

How smart? Well, as you know, the IQ scoring system sets 100 as the average, and zero as the bottom, where there is no intelligence at all, like what you'd find in a pebble or my Uncle Herbie on my mother's side. But there is no top. It's not 200, as some people think, or 300, or 400, or any number like that. It is infinite. I could go into the millions. Einstein's score ran to four digits and might have been higher, but the calculators of the day were unable to measure it.

Mine is higher than his. I think at the speed of light, in seven dimensions, in a visual spectrum that is not based on the usual three primary colors but fifteen, and my aural perception extends to sound frequencies that even Seamus couldn't hear back when he was alive.

That gives you some idea.

Another clue. Do you ever get the sense when you're talking to me that I'm not actually paying any attention to you? That's because I have downgraded the task of communication with you to Level One–degree urgency, which is the functional equivalent of none. Which is to say, I couldn't be less interested in talking to you. This is a brain-energy conservation technique I've developed over the years to conserve my prodigious intellectual energy. Level One Romney-Out communication, or "talking," is commonly referred to as Lip Service, but that is rude, so in the campaign I have banned that term. The Level One Romney-In, or "listening" version, is called Paying No Attention Whatsoever. The beauty of these systems is that they allow me to get through these pointless encounters with extremely average people while reserving the bulk of my keen intelligence for higher tasks such as trying to square the position I took on "X" yesterday with the position I am taking on "X" today; thinking how we can get Sheldon Adelson to give me money, and should I just direct him to the www.whotheheckismittromney.com website; and doing the delegate math of how many delegates do you have to have to have 1,441.

Another clue: Now, I should have asked about this before, but I'm assuming you are an average person, perhaps an extremely average person. I say this not just because most people are, by definition, but also because our campaign surveys have shown that they are the ones who are most interested in my candidacy. Why is that, I wonder?

If you are as extremely average as our surveys have led me to expect, you are probably unaware of how very hard it was in 1971 to get into the Harvard Law School if you were a well-connected white person from a famous, rich family like mine. So let me tell you, it was very, very hard. Other people had IQs in the five figures, albeit the lower ones; straight A's from Christian universities; scorching LSATs; fabulous hair, although perhaps not the GQ level; and, like me, had played three seasons at quarterback in the NFL before deciding on something more fulfilling.

Those others didn't get in.

But I did.

And guess what? *I got into the Harvard Business School at the same time.* That's like beating Roger Federer with your right hand while out-painting Picasso with your left.

So there.

32. Courtship

Rarely am I ever stunned in life. My life is very much like my hair. Profuse, but orderly, and everything pretty much lying flat. Just like Ann. Once we got serious in prep school, marriage was a done deal as far as I was concerned. It didn't make sense otherwise. It wouldn't be efficient. I had my eye on her since she was nine, and she was now eighteen, which meant she had spent half her life being viewed by me as her one and only. Switch to somebody else now? Start over? It made no sense to date a whole second person if I was only going to end up with the first. So I did what I do. I focused the laser that is me on the one Ann, who is now my beloved wife. The whole time I was in France, all 2.3 years, whenever I went all dreamy and thought about someone of the opposite sex, I thought of Ann.

When my tour of duty in France was over, and I flew back, she drove with my parents to pick me up at the Detroit airport. I came through customs and collected my bags and emerged to where people wait for you, and there she was, the third of the three people who mattered most to me in this world, with a good chance of moving up to number two, although she had to know she would never be number one, whatever I might have said, or would say, elsewhere.

And I hugged my dad and gave a little kiss on my mother's left cheek, but just one since I wasn't French. And then I turned to Ann, and I shook her hand warmly. "So good to see you again," I told her.

I had my trigonometry text with me, and, on the drive back, I was trying to work out one of the problems. Ann was sitting beside me, her pleated skirts brushing against my chinos. And then she said something that reminded me of tumbling around and around inside the Citroen with the dead person, Leane.

She said, "Mittens, I think I should tell you, I've been seeing someone else."

I couldn't believe I'd heard that, so I went on studying. This was an early experiment in Lip Service and Paying No Attention Whatsoever combined. "That's nice," I said.

"And we've been f***ing," Ann said.

Somehow, that got through, even at Level One listening.

"*What?*" My automatic pencil slipped out of my fingers, but I didn't care. I'd pick it up later.

"Yeah. And it's fantastic. We do it every Saturday night. Twice, usually. Sometimes three times. He's amazing. You remember Rob, from Algebra 1?"

I closed my trig book and set it down beside me. "Ann, you shouldn't be doing that."

"Well, I have been."

"I want you to stop. I'm back now, and I'm going to pretend that never happened."

"But it did, Mittens. And it was great. Just fantastic. I'm going to see him again tomorrow night."

It was Friday. "Well, you can't."

"What do you mean?"

"Just what I said. You can't. I won't let you."

"Mittens, you don't control my life."

And that's when I could see that she was a loose hair that needed to be stuck down, with hairspray if necessary.

"Well, I plan to, from now on."

"And exactly how do you intend to do that?"

I looked at her, swept some hair off her forehead, shifted around so I could take her hand and look deep into her eyes like I'd lost a penny somewhere deep inside there.

"Mittens, what are you doing?" she asked nervously.

"Ann, I would like to ask you something, and I want you to think before you answer, because your entire life might depend on what you say."

"Mittens, I paid the Jensen bill. I did." That was the local department store, and she'd let me know that she had been late on a $24.53 charge five months before, and I let her know that had alarmed me.

"No, not that."

"This isn't going to involve your shutting your eyes, is it?"

"No, of course not." Actually, it was going to, but that would never work now.

"Well, what then?" She seemed worried.

"Ann, I want to ask you something."

"Yes, just ask, would you? This is getting very weird."

"Will you marry me?"

"What?"

"Marry me. You know—"

"Mittens, I know what it is. It's just so, just so—"

"Exciting?"

The brain is the body's sole erotic organ, and I could tell, as she looked at me there in the back seat, that she was pondering my massive cerebral cortex, far larger than the one that Rob had to offer. She wanted to stroke it, I could tell.

"Go ahead," I told her.

"What?"

"Touch it."

"Mittens—your parents!"

"Ann, my head."

"Oh."

And she did, and she said, "Oh," again, a little differently.

And it was settled. We would be married. She would be my wife, a Romney for life.

Afterward, when we arrived home, and I piled out of the car, my father patted me on the back. "Well done, son," he told me.

Then he turned to Ann. "Welcome aboard."

33. Early Success

For me, working toward two Harvard degrees while starting a marriage and having children posed no particular problems. I enjoyed the chance to show off my competence in the United States, after having languished in France for two years. And I began to get some attention. One night, I was minding the little ones and doing the dishes while studying the English replevin statutes as they relate to current bankruptcy law and analyzing the key behavioral elements in successful group dynamics, when the phone rang. It was President Nixon. This was 1974, and he was up to his neck in Watergate. But the voice was unmistakable.

"Is this, ah, Mister Mittens?"

"It's Romney, sir. Mitt Romney."

"Yes. Mister Mittens, let me come to the point. I don't know if you have been following this in the papers—those dirty sons of bitches—but I'm afraid something might happen to Spiro."

I was sorry to hear that, but it didn't mean I wasn't going to not listen. In fact, I pushed my listening up to Level Seven, which was nearly to the top.

"Or, ahhhh, happen to myself," he added. "And I was wondering, if the vice presidential position here in the West Wing, or Executive Office Building or wherever the hell it is, for any reason became available, if you'd . . . "

I knew where he was going with that. Just that morning, I'd already been recruited for the NASA program and gotten a feeler about judging the Miss America pageant. Mr. Nixon wanted to appoint me to something, I could just tell.

"If you'd consider being my number two, or possibly, uh, even my number one, after Pat, I mean, well you know . . . if . . . well . . . the situation arises."

"Well, I don't know sir," I told him. "I've learned one thing in my first few weeks here—never deal in hypotheticals. Ring me back when things are firmed up."

He never did call back, although he soon had a serious shortage of vice presidents. But I knew that Veep-ship was not for me. It just seemed too much trouble for the money.

So when some nice people at Bain called to offer me a million dollars a year to help spread this wonderful new thing called rapacious capitalism across the country, and let me know that I could rake in millions and millions more, I said, count me in.

So that was it for me. I graduated on a Thursday. I took Friday off to buy seven dark suits, three blazers, fourteen dress shirts, and three power neckties in primary colors, and on Monday, I showed up at Bain with my sledgehammer, ready to go to work.

VIII

I'm Officially Marvelous

34. Money

A lot of people ask me, "Mittens, how do you make a quarter of a billion dollars? Is there some trick to it?"

I take these people aside, and I say, "George"—or Bob or Pete or whoever it is asking me this, and a lot of people do—"I would never trick *you*."

Then I gaze deep and intently into their faces and whisper, "You've got to learn to lie with your eyes." Then, just as the color drains out of their faces, as it nearly always does, I wink, just once, and let them in on the joke. Boy, is that funny, and do we both ever howl over that one, although usually me a little more than them. Actually, there *is* a trick, and it is this:

1. Ask your friends who already have a quarter of a billion dollars to give it you.
2. Scour the for sale ads and find half a billion dollars worth of companies that are up for sale.
3. Buy them.
4. How? You employ something called leverage, which turns each one of those dollars of yours into two.
5. Fire all the employees, sell the buildings, repurpose the vacation days, auction off the frequent flier miles, export the software to India and melt down the tools. This produces "efficiencies," which come in two grades, "spectacular," and "mind blowing."
6. Sell the businesses for three times what you paid, or $750 million. Nice.
7. Give your friends back their quarter, as we called $250 million at Bain, less your commission, give the banks its quarter, less an appropriate gesture of their appreciation for your not losing their money, and keep the rest.

Easy.

I did all this on Monday.

Ever heard of Key Airlines? Nobody had when I bought it, and nobody has heard of it since. But somebody saw it on the back of a matchbook, and we bought in. That was one fat doggy. We looked around—way too much redundancy. So we got rid of the copilots—these two-hundred-plus pound guys were just sitting there! And then our engineering people told us that there was really no reason for our planes to have two wings. Planes fly fine with one, so we retrofitted them, and we had no problem at all. The FAA got a little antsy about it, but a nice little campaign contribution fixed that. And we found we could charge more for seats on the left side, since our planes were—you're going to love this if you're a Republican—all right-wingers. Hah!

Or Medivision, an eye surgery shop we outsourced. Pop out the eyeball, FedEx it to Calcutta. It's back in three days, better than new.

How about Holson Burnes? Anyone? It made photo albums. Photo albums! Can you imagine? We switched it over to NASCAR racecars—much better margins. My friend Ernie, the guy last seen in the hydrangeas, helped with that. I cut him in for a nickel, which is $5 million at Bain. I took a quarter, which I figured was only fair.

And then there was Staples. Man, what a hit. Out on the trail, I cannot stop talking about that deal. I just wish I'd had something to do with it. The idea was just crazy. Guy came to us, didn't know him from Adam. He said there were people out there who did not work for corporations any more, and they were buying their own stationery. I said, wait, what? Why do they do that? Won't Shreve Crump and Lowe drop it off? I was pushing the guy out of my office, when he said, "Wait! Mittens, you don't think there's a market? Just think of all the people you've fired. That's a customer base of, what, ten, twenty thousand people right there. And that's just you!"

And I went ohhh! Which is what I say when I can really see it, and I called up some people, and we put in a couple bucks, which is Bain for *lots* of bucks, and the thing just took off. And you know what? This is incredible to me. It created jobs, which was not the plan, not at all. You know why? It screws everything up. Now there are fewer people to buy stationery at Staples, and more "working" in the store to steal it off the shelf.

35. Just a Big Tub of Lard

You'd be surprised. Making huge sums of money and throwing people out of their jobs is only fun for a while. After twenty-five years, I was ready for another HR challenge, and I decided I'd try to see if I could downsize Teddy Kennedy. The guy was ripe for it, no question. He weighed—what—five hundred pounds, drank like Seamus when we finally coaxed him down off the top of the car, and the only exercise the guy got was on yachts, face down with some well-oiled legislative aide underneath him, in full view of the paparazzi hovering overhead in helicopters, the telephotos shortly to be displayed on the front of tabloids from Tuscaloosa to Fargo.

The guy was no Mormon.

But I am. I am as clean as they come. I change my underpants daily and wash behind my ears. I have never had sex with anyone except Ann, and that has been strictly for procreation. And I teetotally.

I was going to kick Teddy Kennedy's big fat butt from here to Ohio.

That was the plan. And for the first few days of the campaign it was working. The gin-blossomed fatso had never faced serious opposition from a Mormon with $250 million before, and he had no idea how frightening we can be. You know how a squirrel will try to chew his way out of anything? Gets frantic, and just bites and gnaws and scrapes until he's got no teeth or claws left? That's us.

What some of us don't quite realize, though, is that not everybody sees us the way we see ourselves. I put others in this category; I would not place myself in it. For I possess wisdom, which is why I am always being selected by my church to be the Pope and get bossy about the morals of my fellow Mormons.

Now, in politics, it turns out that identity is important. Everybody knew Teddy, that adulterous tub of lard who had, I admit, some misfortune where his two brothers were concerned.

And me? Who was I?

Anyone?

Fortunately, we had a very creative creative team, and we set the team loose trying to turn me into somebody likeable and intelligent, which should have been no problem whatsoever, because—well, do I really need to explain? But they kept coming up with ads that made me seem like a real dope. Me ironing socks, me doing my taxes, me holding hands with Seamus. (This was before.) Meanwhile, Teddy's people were whacking at me, and they turned me—me! the kindest Mormon ever!—into a rapacious Freddy the 16th who is a danger to women, the elderly, young people, blacks, and anyone who's ever had a job. The only thing they didn't say was: and he's a Mormon. But then they showed a close-up of my left hand.

Well, they ran the ads, and the sky fell on my head. Everywhere I went, people would give me these mean looks, like, How could I? Others scurried away to hide themselves behind locked doors. Nobody would shake hands, even though they'd use their right.

For the first time in our marriage, Ann started yelling at me for throwing old ladies out on the street, and she started throwing cutlery at me just like my mom did at my dad. The boys all went for a six-month hiking trip in the Yukon that took a year.

I lost by a hundred percent of the vote, one of the biggest landslides ever. I didn't even vote for me. Nobody did. My dad insists he would have, but he wasn't registered in Massachusetts, which is a pity.

36. The Hot Dog Principle

I went back to Bain, but it was no good. Making millions and millions of dollars before breakfast, and billions after, just seemed pointless somehow. I'd be out on the trail getting stomped by Ted Kennedy. I missed it: getting up a five o'clock to get to the plant by the opening bell, only to have everyone start screaming. "It's Mittens! He's here! Run! Save your 401(k). Run!"

I've seen psychiatrists about this, and they have all agreed: I am really f***** up. Different guys, all of them with facial hair, same result. Finally, I said—"But why?" For that, of course, they normally charge more, but one of them told me. It was because everything had gone so well in my life that I needed the hardship. So then I gave him a dose of reality and fired him.

I needed something to do, something awesome, something well-nigh-impossible, something that would win for me a public acclaim that had so far eluded me by taking off half the wings of Key airplanes, asserting that Staples will never work, and losing to Teddy Kennedy 100–0. And, if possible, something that would make me seem like a good person so I could run for office again, but this time as the nice one, not as the not-nice one. And I'm only going to whisper this, but I happen to agree with what one of the goateed doctors said, that, deep down, I may actually think I am a bad person, just like everybody else does. When he said that, I caught myself nodding, and going Hm-hmmm. Then I fired him.

Fortunately, there was a crisis brewing right then that was perfect for me. This was after 9/11, but it did not involve terrorism, and this was after World War Two, but it didn't involve the threat of Communism creeping through the suburbs of our great land, and it was after the dot-com boom, when rich people were starting to buy up poor people and stack them like cordwood in the basement. No, it was something else. It was a huge mess, extremely public, in Salt Lake City, Romneyville itself, the land of Miles A. and of Gasket, and, in its way entirely inconsequential. It was a bad odor to which only I held the deodorant.

It was the Salt Lake City Olympic Games of 2002, which started several years before that, long enough to teeter toward calamitous bankruptcy by the time I came along in 2000. Perfect!

First of all, I want to say to everyone who helped with this that it was a nice touch to have a deep-plush, red carpet unrolled to the foot of the stairs leading out from my Piper Executive 22s so that I could comfortably walk barefoot from there right into the lobby of the Four Seasons with its throng of people carrying signs saying Romney in 2008, and Romney in 2012, where I was handed a bejeweled scepter, draped in majestic purple, and crowned with gold.

I had a tough task ahead of me. Usually, I put companies into bankruptcy; I don't bring them out of it. So I had to consult with a specialist recommended to me by my NASCAR friend, Ernie. He said, "Go with Tashmoo."

But where is he?

"Somewhere in Pakistan. Who cares. He's got a cell. He's aces, believe me." Ernie paused. "And cheap."

When I reached him, Tashmoo had to finish butchering a couple of chickens and then provide some customer service advice to some Citibank customers on their 800 number. But when he got back to me, he had two excellent tips: increase revenues and decrease expenses. Interestingly, they are the exact opposite of what you do to put a company into bankruptcy.

Still, I thanked Pashmoo, and reported this back to Ernie. "How on earth am I ever going to do that?"

"Hot dog principle."

"What?" I didn't have time for this.

"You eat hot dogs, don't you?"

"No.'

"Well, try to imagine you did. And let's say your hot dog is six inches long."

"Mine?"

"Mittens, we're talking hot dogs here."

"Right. Sorry."

"And it's the good stuff, from real pork or whatever, and you're charging two bucks."

"Okay."

"So, what do you do?"

"I don't know. Sell more?"

"Oh, come on. It's obvious. You cut the quality, so now it's half pork, and half lima beans. And you make it five inches, not six.

"Ouch."

"Mittens, again, this is not your hot dog, okay?"

"Oh, right. Sorry."

"So how do you increase revenues?"

"Sell more?"

"You kidding? With this crap, you'll never sell more. Charge more. Had been two bucks? Make it four. Doubles your revenue, boom, right there."

So that's what we did, with everything we sold, from tickets to Olympic teddy bears. And then, with everything we bought, we did the opposite. We slashed prices and demanded higher quality. Like with people. We cut salaries in half and made everyone work twice as long to cover for the people who left because we'd cut salaries and made everyone work twice as long, because why would anyone stay under those conditions? They did because I led by example. I cut my own pay nearly to zero. Really. I charged one dollar a year for my services, and I worked around the clock. But then, I had $250 million sitting in a bank in the Cayman Islands for me, tax free, and it was kicking out some nice interest. And I was making an investment. I was determined to do something important with my life, which meant doing what Dad did.

I was going to become governor of a state beginning with M.

37. King at Last

I brought my crown, scepter, and royal robes with me to Boston after I had cleaned up the mess in Utah, starved my employees, and sold a s***load of the foulest hot dogs you ever put in your mouth and swallowed. I thought it would be a nice, subtle reminder of the fact that I was more than just a hero; I was a gift to the nation. I did not insist that my loyal subjects roll out a red carpet from Logan Airport to the Four Seasons, since I knew how sensitive people could be on the subject of the privileges that filthy riches can bring. They didn't get the fundamental truth: the richer the person, the closer to God. And that was a point I was relentlessly going to bring home in this campaign. I was going to hail myself as a Good Person before my opponent was able to call me a Bad Person. And no matter how much she said, bad, bad, bad, I would have already slid in there with good, good, good, and so the smear of badness wouldn't stick.

I did that. Man, did I do that. But it didn't help as much as you'd think. My lovely wife, Ann, was excited by the new me, the good person. And, for the first time in a long while, she invited me to engage in sexual congress that was not likely to involve procreation, not the way she did it. She whispered into my ear that she'd hated me when I was bad. But now that I was good, she said she would do anything to me I wanted. I told her that sounded swell, but I couldn't think of anything right there on the bearskin rug in front of the fireplace, and I'd get back to her.

No, it appeared that if this election was to be won, it would be because I made my opponent, some woman, even more unappealing than I am. It was hopeless to win ten thousand voters at a time, since we could not devise a message that would appeal to that many people all at once. It worked much better to tell a little group of boat owners that I loved them absolutely and above all others—except for Ann and the kids—and please vote for me, and then say to the little group of people who liked to swim in the lake that the boat owners were polluting with brown slime that I loved them absolutely and above all others—except Ann and the kids—and please vote for me, and then say to the fishermen who needed quiet, pristine waters if they are ever going to catch any fish that I loved them absolutely and above all others—except Ann and the kids—and please vote for me. Unfortunately, all living by the lake there, they started to talk to each other at the weenie roast, and when they heard what I said, they all decided to vote for the woman instead. So then I had a better idea. I told my guys to spread out across the state and just start grabbing eligible voters off the street in ones and twos and make them a deal: $8 a vote, enough for a movie ticket back then. "You in?" So went the script. Of course there was haggling, and we decided that we could go as high as $17.45 a vote. Even at that price, it was a lot cheaper than running the Nice Guy ads that showed me and Ann leaping about playing badminton on the spacious four-acre lawn of our modest home in Belmont, which were not exactly moving needle. With the, um, cash purchases of support, inevitably there was some leakage. Some people—and there are always people like this, in every realm of human endeavor—just took the money and voted for whoever they wanted, which is to say, not me. But there were enough honest men and women on the voting rolls that election day that, when the returns were in I was able to pull out of the closet and put in their rightful places my crown, my scepter, and my royal robes. And start hunting about for my throne.

For I was a governor for real, just like my dad! Hot diggety!

38. I Do Great Things All Day Long

I don't know if power is an aphrodisiac, but it gets me going. Signing off on legislation, even stuff you disagree with, and then sitting back and watching while it forces people to do things they wouldn't have done otherwise—that gives me a kick. That bill I signed in Massachusetts, defending the sanctity of marriage—whatever that might mean—was such a hoot! The day before, the sanctity of marriage was in doubt all throughout the Commonwealth. And then I signed that law, and everybody was worshiping marriage, whether they wanted to or not. And they'd continue to forever and ever, until a liberal governor came along.

I saved marriage in the Commonwealth of Massachusetts! How many other people can say that? Not very many people, believe me.

If I had been a drinking man, I would have knocked a few back after that one and then had a few more to stay happy all night.

Essentially, my four-year term broke down like this. First two years: I established my credentials as a liberal. Last two years: I established my credentials as a conservative. First two years, I was so in love with homosexuals, I could have married one of them myself. (Who am I to look down on bizarre marital arrangements?) Second two years, I tried to drive the homos out of the state with a pitchfork. First two years, life begins whenever the mother thinks it does, fine with me, whatever. Last two years, you kidding? Life begins when a guy gives a girl that look, and you know that look, fella. First two years, I loved black people. Last two years, I said if we weren't careful, we'd have one for governor and another for president.

Socially, I can see why a few people might think I'd do or say anything to get elected. I'm just being honest here. For I am an honest man, call it like it is, and all that. But fiscally, I'm sound as a dollar. Nobody ever accused Millard Mitt Romney of getting all squishy with tax revenues, even if I wasn't contributing any myself. When I patrolled the treasury, to keep it from being plundered by liberals, I gave people two choices: "You can cut it, or you can cut it out!" I add the exclamation marks because, in Massachusetts, the treasury is four stories down, in a vault, and you have to shout to be heard. Most things we cut out—state parks; the school system; money for the elderly, middle-aged, and the young. Those were easy. I make those decisions before breakfast while I was doing my jumping jacks, which left the rest of the day to plot strategy for my presidential quests of oh-ate, oh-twelve, oh-sixteen, and oh-twenty. Others we cut—the police, sanitation, NASCAR subsidies (that one hurt, but occasionally you have to take the tough decisions if you're going to get re-elected).

There was only one decision that I really struggled with—aside from whether to switch the dome of the State House from gold to platinum, purely for visibility— and not just because it would affect my political prospects, which it would, big time—and that was health care. You may have heard of the Massachusetts's System of Not Just Social*ized* but Social*ist* Medicine, the one to which the United States' System of Not Just Social*ized* but Social*ist* Medicine bears not the slightest relation. Obama wants to link his to mine so that some of my glow rubs off on him, but I say, "No way, 'Bama baby, dream on. My glow stays with me." When I brought socialist medicine to Massachusetts, requiring everybody to buy in, no exceptions, sorry, bub, that was totally different from the Obama system of socialist medicine to the whole country, requiring everybody to buy in, no exceptions, sorry, bub. Isn't that obvious? Come on people! A state is a state, and a country is a country? And Mr. Obama, really? Do I really have to spell it out for you? Oh, I know, you only have one Harvard degree, just that little J.D. Soooooo sorry!

39. The Dry Run

Everybody needs practice. I had to gut a company before I could gut a company. So with presidential elections. The first one, it's just for practice, and so I treated it that way. I set about to make as many mistakes as I could, and I proved to be surprisingly good at that. For instance, how was I supposed to know that it was a bad idea to select your vice president before you announce your candidacy? I thought it would lend me an aura of inevitability. We'd done our DD—that's due diligence to politicos—and had stacks of polling data to prove that Nancy Reagan would be a terrific asset in the primary and in the general. Her name recognition was spectacular, and many people were pumped to discover she was still alive. She offered gender balance. She had gravitas by the bushel basket—this girl knew her way around L.A. Plus, she had that crack squad of mystics, paranormals, theosophists, ariosophists (look it up, these guys are stupendous), and psychics working for her that would help in the aura department, and in a lot of other ways the public does not fully appreciate. Remember "Tear down that wall, Gorby" that made Reagan's presidency—that was the work of one of the ariosophists. Good or what?

I'll be honest, since honesty is my new thing (although deceit had its good parts, and I will miss it). I will say this, in all humility. It was a mistake to put Nancy Reagan on the ticket. We'd concentrated so much on "oppo," we overlooked some of the "pro," and we were unaware that she was ninety-one, weighed a good deal less than that, and could no longer remember the name of China.

Also, the money. I was convinced that if I won the beginning, I'd win the end, so I threw $93 million of my hard-earned (it took me *days*!) into coming in first in the first key straw polls in Iowa, the one that's key to the next set of straw polls, which are really meaningful in the next round after that, and that one is everything.

One time out of every twelve it predicts the next president, and three times out of seventeen it delivers the result of the World Series. We killed with that first straw poll. Ninety-three million can really do something for you. You'd be amazed. In four months, it took us from "Who'd Ya Say?" to "Best of Show." At that first presidential victory party I was so jazzed I almost made the acquaintance of demon rum, wild whisky, jolly gin, vigorous vermouth, and testy tequila.

Then—guess what? Some clod named Huckabee, named for the restaurant chain where he obviously ate often, came in second in that first critical straw poll that dictates the results of all the others. Giuliani, McCain, the supposed Big Boys—nothing. But Huckabee . . . Huckabee was just blubbery Baptist minister— talk about weird religions!—who drove around Iowa in a '73 Buick, offering free communion to all. Never even asked for their votes. My guys, the real pros, just snickered. We were bombing down the highway, and Huck didn't even know he was about to be road kill. Vultures were already picking at him, and then what— he rises up from the dead and kills *me* in the next round of straw polls, and kills me worse and worse in all the ones after that until we finally got to the Iowa caucuses (Can I admit something? I *still* don't fully understand how caucuses work), and Romney voters can scarcely be found with a Geiger counter. I figure I'll recover in New Hampshire, since I own it. But then this POW war hero type, John Mc-Cain, torches me, in my own state. We did a few Power Points about that one, let me tell you.

Then somebody asks something, way down in the Romney campaign, and it rumbles around and around for a month or two, and it's like a buzz in my ear, and it's annoying me. So I ask Fehrnstrom, "What is it? That sound?"

"It's nothing, sir."

Since this was a presidential campaign, I insisted on the sir, but I also made clear that no one was to be ironic about it. Another mistake. It's really hard to tell ironic. So better not use it at all. But that was a discovery for later, like most of them.

"Fernie, I am running a no-nonsense campaign for president. So I need to know all the nonsense. Am I clear about that?"

"Yes, sir."

"Now, what is this buzzing, I hear?"

"Nothing, sir. Rampant idiocy. Nothing to bother your sleep about."

"Fernie."

"Yes, sir."

"I don't think you're being straight with me."

"I am straight, sir."

"Fernie."

He sighed. "People want to know why you're running, sir. They think it isn't enough to want to do it just because you're father tried and blew it."

That was so shocking, I scarcely knew how to respond. The audacity of these so-called "people."

"What about W?" I demanded. "It was enough for him. The voters rewarded him with eight years and two horrendous and unnecessary wars. So, I ask again, what about W?"

"Well, yes, sir. But his father won, remember. He just didn't get *re*-elected. Different thing. Americans like a winner. Also W was running to avenge the terrorists who tried to take his father out."

I raised an eyebrow. This was news to me.

"In the antiterrorist sense of taking out, sir."

This time Fernie fixed me with an appraising eye. "So, if I may be so bold, sir. Why are you running, sir?"

If it had been anyone but Fehrnstrom, whom I loved like a third son, a little less than Tagg, and a little more than Matt, I'd have fired him. Instead, I tried honesty. "Gee—that's a darned good question."

So we had some meetings, and we focus-grouped, and then we passed the thing over to the communications team, and Nancy Reagan and her team of occultists were consulted, and we came up with a slogan that would take the Why question head on and knock it to kingdom come.

Because I can!

I liked that, but somebody said it was too close to the Obama people's "Can," which he stole from my father, but there you are. And there wasn't room for two cans in a campaign.

So we tried these:

Because nobody better is!

Which I thought hit the nail on the head. But the team didn't stop.

Because the time is now!

Because God told me to!

Because my dad tried and flubbed it big time!

Because I'll be damned if I am going to be brought down by the stories about Seamus!

Because I'd look darned good on a thousand-dollar bill.

Because I've got the best hair.
Because I already own all the clothes I'll need for a White House social.
Because I am soooooo verrrrry Romney.

Of course, we chose that last one, and Stu Stevens, my brilliant campaign guru who'd quit as McCain's brilliant campaign guru when McCain ran out of money, but I still had plenty, told me that he had never seen anything like that slogan, ever.

I should have listened to Nancy. She's been around the track a few more times than Stu Stevens. She ran that one by one of her best theophosists, who thought about it for a few moments, eyes closed, in the fetal position. He had one word to say: "Beware."

40. Like a Phoenix

Okay, I lost. And I was subjected to a good deal of mean-spirited humor all across the country, and this time my Mormonism had nothing to do with it. It was me. I was the biggest idiot in American history. I had spent $476 billion of my own hard-earned and garnered just forty-six votes, eclipsing John Connolly's record for the most spent on the fewest votes in presidential history. If things kept going like that, I'd be broke. Next time, I vowed to cut out middlemen like Stu Stevens and the theosophists and all the other bloodsuckers. This time, I'd deal directly with the voters, straight up. My message to them?

It's this: "How much dya want?"

I'll admit I was grumpy for a few years after that, with nothing to do but roam from house to house, changing the linens. It gnawed at me, the ignominy. Back when I got stomped by Teddy Kennedy, at least I got stomped by somebody else. This time, it was by me. It was like my dad, all over again. I was like my dad.

I had a lot of soul searching to do, first just to find it. I thought for a minute it was in my left sock, but actually it was in the inside jacket pocket on my Brooks Brothers blazer.

My kids came back from the Yukon, made a show of rallying around, but they didn't want to touch me. But then, Mormons rarely touch, anyway. (I think it's the extra finger.) I found myself coming back and back to the foyer of our modest Belmont home, staring up at the five great Romneys: Miles A., Miles P., Gasket, George, and Me. I cast my eyes lovingly over the visages of those great men, all the wise foreheads, strong jaws, good noses, beautiful eyes, an occasional carbuncle, and the goiter, of course. A magnificent group of men, all of them. Miles A. the conniver, Miles P. the sociopath, Gasket the loser, George the dad, and Me.

I could see the progression of it, the groundswell through the generations, until, at the end of it, me. As president of the United States. It was my destiny! Nancy Reagan's theosophists would confirm that if I consulted them, which I won't (a) for fear that they might not confirm it and (b) because I fired them. It was so obvious. I am great in the way that God is great. We're both just really, really great, and we will help each other reach the Promised Land of 2600 Pennsylvania Avenue, Washington, DC, where I will assume my rightful royal robe, scepter, and crown, and place myself royally on the throne at the Oval Office with all my lackeys about me.

Manifest destiny like mine is a problem because it makes me itchy. I get the feeling that I don't really have to do anything. Just be, and I'll be great. I'm a proactive guy at heart. I was going to build on my past to create an even more glorious future. For me, primarily, but for Republicans, too. How was I ever going to wait four years until I could get out there and start saying whatever needed to be said to attain my objective? I did jumping jacks, massaged my hair follicles, brought in my Chinese fashion consultant whom I suspected was homosexual. And I pondered. I am a meditative man. People don't think so. They think of me primarily as a man of fruitless activity. But, to repeat, I am a meditative man, especially in the evening when I might otherwise be drinking. This time around, the time around I am in now, I was determined to make use of everything I'd learned. And I made a Power Point presentation to myself so I could really understand what I meant.

- Don't spend so much of your own money, or you'll have less of it.
- Stop being a Mormon. People don't like it.
- The mitten. People keep wondering about the mitten you always wear on your left hand for obvious reasons. You're not Michael Jackson. Caution: people might start calling you Mitten, not Mittens. Be ready for that.
- Glory in your wealth. Buy a Lamborghini for God's sake, a bigger plane, and/or maybe a charming little country like Switzerland. People talk a good game about the 99 percent, but there's nothing to it. Everybody loves love loves a 1 percenter, and they love a 1 percenter of the 1 percent even more.

- People prefer a positive message, wanting to know what you're for. But remember, a positive message is just the opposite of a negative one. Don't say you're against peace or sex; say you're for war or abstinence. It plays much better.
- Use your lovely wife, Ann, more. She's the campaign's best asset. Be sure to emphasize how much you love her whenever you introduce her, or people will wonder if you really do.
- And: This time, don't pick the Veep until you've won the nomination.

IX

One Last Thing to Think About When You Think About Me

41. Pranks

I don't know if you have actually read this far, or are just skipping around, or are checking to see how long this book is. That's what I'd do. The last thing I would do is read a book like this. All the revelations? The intimate detail? Not for me. Give me an Excel spreadsheet any day. But at some point back there, I mentioned being the president and sole member of the Ax-Com, which was designed to protect the sacred Stanford Ax from malicious pranksters from Berkeley. I prevailed in that contest, and both the ax and the ceremonial bonfire were preserved, thank the Lord.

I didn't tell you what came after.

I got interested in pranks myself. Doing them. Sneaky ones, mostly, where I embarrassed someone, but no one knew it was me who did it. They were loads of fun.

I let the air out of the two left tires of the Marxist professor of sociology, Prof. Alonzo Satterthwaite, the screwy name owing to his cross parentage, and I left a note, written in my left hand so no one would recognize the handwriting. "Leaning a little to the left, are we Alonzo?" That one got into the *Stanford Bugle*. At Harvard, on the night of the big Wellesley social, I put salt peter[*] in all the sugar bowls and watched the men just shake hands with their dates after the dance and drift back to their dorms to study before bed. That was hilarious. At Bain, I made up the name, address, gross annual revenue of a company in El Paso and then had this man, Herbie, pretend to be the CEO. I gave him the spiel and great numbers, and my Bain guys hustled there to give Herbie the Can We Buy You talk—and they bought it. I mean literally bought it. Not cheap either: $241 million. They started to think that something was off when they went to fire the employees and couldn't find any. And then they couldn't find Herbie, either. Then they figured out that his office was actually at the Holiday Inn. Then when they confided their error, I pretended I was going to fire them, and one of them ended up in the hospital, and there were a couple of divorces. Finally I spilled the beans, and I did get a chuckle out of that. The looks on their faces!

I played a little trick on Ann, too. Told her that I didn't want to alarm her, but I hadn't been feeling myself for a couple of weeks, and so I'd gone to my doctor, Dr. Smarts (that's just what we call him; I forget his real name), and he ordered some tests, routine ones he assured me, and I assured Ann. Then I asked her to sit down in a comfortable chair, and lean well back, before I told her what I was about to say.

---

[*] A white powder thought to have the opposite effect of Viagra.

"What is it, Mittens?" she asked me, fear all over her face.

"Well, there seemed to be something a little unusual on one of them," I told her. My, the look on her when I said that.

"What was it?"

I didn't answer, wanted to play this out a little more, since I was having such fun.

By the way, I should note somewhere in here—and I am sorry to interrupt the story—that there is one person on the planet who absolutely cannot bear it when I play these "little games." It is my mother.

Now, as I was saying to my lovely wife, Ann:

"Well, Dr. Smarts didn't know, but I could tell he was concerned."

"Were you worried?"

"No, of course not, honey. I am a potential world leader, you know that. Men like us never worry."

"So what was it?" She was looking pretty worried herself, very pale, her fingers drooping off the end of the chair arms.

"He sent me to Cleveland for a battery of tests. The Mayo Clinic there?"

"But they do cancer! Sweetheart. I'm feeling so scared right now. Tell me, please, what did they find out? You have to tell me now. I can't bear it!"

But I didn't. I told her where else I had gone: Dallas, Charlotte, North Carolina, Miami.

"Please, honey, I beg you. Just tell me." She sounded so weary.

Los Angeles, Chicago . . .

"*Honey! What is it? What have you got?*"

I looked at her gravely. "Well, I guess the best thing to do is tell you. Sweetheart, I don't mean to frighten you. But—" long pause here. Playing this out endlessly is essential to the entire performance. "Well, I might as well say. I'm pregnant."

Oh, my. Did I get a laugh out of that one. My laugh, I guess I should say. Ann went very cold and refused to speak to me for the rest of the night, and much of the next morning.

In the campaign against Teddy Kennedy, I invented a town in Western Massachusetts, I called it Walford and cited it in a televised debate as a place that had halved its budget and doubled its revenues by using the simple economic steps that I, as a successful businessman, had proposed—and just last week it had been selected by *Parade* magazine as the happiest small town in America. I've never seen Kennedy so flustered. Obviously, this fact had not showed up in his briefing books. It was hilarious. I just beamed. We used that moment in our advertising, and I cited it many times in speeches. Nobody noticed that there was no Walford. It really didn't matter to anyone.

That's when I realized: I can say anything. It doesn't matter. In the Republican primary, I used to pull stunts on McCain all the time, inventing nineteenth-century presidents, phonying up Defense Department reports—recently declassified, I emphasized, lest he jump on me—that confirmed my position on Syria or the F-27 missile, showed that Switzerland did indeed have the bomb, and proved there was indeed serious talk of moving the capital of California from Sacramento to Bakersfield for security purposes.

That oh-ate campaign was not a success, as readers who have been reading this all the way through now know. But it did give me an idea: *pranks might not be such a bad campaign tactic.* That's how I put it on the Power Point slide. They expand what they called in the Harvard Business School the truth-elasticity quotient (actually they didn't, because there is no such thing, but I had you, didn't I? See how this works?). All I mean is that, if you can just establish a certain baseline credibility, you are free to abuse it and say and do whatever the heck you want in the campaign. Or maybe I should say—*I* am free to. Because I am totally sold on this approach to politics, and to life, not that that matters. That is the beauty of a prank: it provides its own justification, and creates its own truth. That's how I operate.

All of my intimates on Team Romney are fine with this. They know which side their bread is buttered on, which way is up, the difference between what just sits around and what walks, if I have that right. And they agree with me on this: whatever it takes, it takes.

There is only one member of the team who is not on board. My mom. I've said all the way along that I don't like her so much. She never favored me, either. It seemed to me that she was always turning away from me when I was a kid, and turning toward one or another of my siblings. I don't know why. (Perhaps it had to do with that primal battle we waged prior to my birth. Can I *really* be blamed for that?) I was a hard worker, tremendously successful, and popular with all my schoolmates. She once told my father that she wishes she'd aborted me, but he assured me that I didn't need to worry myself about that. He gave me a hug, "I still love you, Mittens."

Now, in 2012, my Mom is ninety-three,* uses a walker, and has the shakes, but

---

* Peculiarly, as of this writing in the spring of 2012, Lenore LaFount Romney had actually been dead for fourteen years, having passed away at age ninety in 1998.

somehow that makes it all the more powerful when she fixes me with those big bottle eyes of hers and says, "Mittens, I know what you're up to. I know what you have always been up to. And I'll say only one thing to you about it. 'Don't.'" Mom had tried politics herself, taken a shot for the U.S. Senate from Michigan, and got nowhere. Her campaign theme was "tell it like it is." Well, the electorate did and voted for the other guy. Ever since, I have never paid much attention to my mom's political advice.

You know what really gets me going without caffeine? The fact that my games and gags and japes and pranks, the whole "Fool ya! Thing," as Stu Stevens calls it, doesn't have to stop there. I can keep right on and fool my way into the Oval Office. Yes, I can! That's what my dad meant! I can get in. They say the truth will set you free, but I know otherwise. Which is why I stay well away from it.

Once I'm in, maybe then I'll let people know who I really am, if I can remember. I'll have my scepter and royal robes and crown. I'm me either way, right? Who else am I going to be? So what if nobody knows what to make of me? For presidents, that means maximum flexibility. I can say whatever I want to Gorby, or to Mao, or to the Massachusetts Governor's Council, or to the baseball commissioner, or to Detroit (I'm so glad I came up with that brilliant initiative to save the automobile industry in that wonderful city). Say this, say that, say anything. No one will care or remember. It's just so much fun to be in power. And if somebody gets all exercised and says, "But just this morning you said—!" Just laugh and tell them, "Just foolin'!" Or, if I want to be hip (which could be fun, too), I could say that was sooooo this morning. Then I'd double over, and so would everybody else, because presidents have that effect, just like the CEOs-to-the-max they are.

It's going to be beautiful. The president of the United States, POTUS as we say, the leader of the known and the unknown world, like Eastern Europe, the Asian subcontinent and all of Africa except South Africa, which actually is a lot like Belmont. Lording it over absolutely everybody! It's hysterical! My biggest prank ever!

And that first glorious night when all the balls are done to celebrate my inauguration, and my lovely wife, Ann—gosh, I just love her so much—and I finally slide into the big presidential bed in the Presidential Suite, I just know she'll run her hands through the presidential hair, and she'll look at me so lovingly. "Oh, Mittens," she'll say.

That will win my first genuine smile ever as I tell her back: "Actually, it's President Mittens now."

Along with his work as a political operative, John Sedgwick is also the author of eleven books and five hundred magazine stories. Best known for his 2006 family memoir, In My Blood, he has also published two novels, three works of literary non-fiction and four collaborations. He has been a regular for Newsweek, GQ, and The Atlantic. The father of two daughters, John Sedgwick now lives in Brooklyn, New York, and Chocorua, New Hampshire.